Christmas Luck

Arizona Heat, Book Four

Hilary Dartt

Also by Hilary Dartt

Arizona Heat

Pure Luck

Sweet Luck

Terrific Luck

Love Under the Arizona Sky

All the Stars

The Whole Sky

To the Moon

Mint Creek Ranch

My Favorite Story

My Favorite View

My Favorite Place

Seedling Homestead

A Summer of Wonder

A Dream of Home

A Promise of Forever

The Intervention Series

The Dating Intervention

The Marriage Intervention

The Motherhood Intervention

The Garden Club Series

Jasmine's Pact

Studying Sequoia

Just Holly

Christmas Luck

Arizona Heat, Book Four

Hilary Dartt

Chapter One

At first, Pearl found being single and alone infinitely better than being married and lonely. After a year, the post-divorce honeymoon phase had worn off.

"Welcome to your new life, Pearl Houston," she said to her reflection one Monday morning in December as she splashed cold water on her face.

Running through her to-do list, she pulled on her clothes for the day—dark jeans and a cashmere sweater she tried to forget her ex-husband gave her four Christmases ago.

Feed Wyatt and Will.

Drop them off at school.

Pray Wyatt doesn't get in trouble. Again.

Call the handyman.

A headache formed as she pulled on her jeans and envisioned shoehorning each item into her packed workday. Not that her boss, June Sterling, was anything other than accommodating, but she was also mere weeks from giving birth and at that point in her pregnancy when, Pearl knew, the baby was wedged between her rib cage and hipbones and it was hard to breathe. Having been there herself, Pearl wanted to do all she could to be helpful.

Which was why the falling apart of nearly every appliance she owned had come at the worst possible time.

She huffed as she slid her sweater over her head, loving the silky-soft fabric on her skin and simultaneously hating that Leslie had given it to her. After the divorce, she'd debated getting rid of it, but she'd lusted after it for months before finally asking for it for Christmas (since Leslie couldn't think of any original ideas and always insisted she give him a list).

A scream pierced the morning quiet and Pearl froze, earring in one hand, earring back in the other, trying to discern whether the scream resulted from injury, anger, frustration, fear, or none of the above.

"You've just sealed your fate of certain death!" Wyatt's holler sounded playful, and Pearl put in her earring.

The boys were engaged—once again—in some kind of battle, and she had about twelve seconds before someone started crying.

"And there it is."

Will wailed for a full two seconds before Pearl heard an angry grunt and a *whack*. Then another shout and the sound of thundering footsteps moved down the hall and stopped at her bedroom door, which flung open to reveal both boys, neither of whom were dressed (and she could have sworn they'd both been fully dressed at breakfast).

After a solid minute of literal finger pointing and more yelling, Pearl felt her eyelids slide closed.

"Take me away," she whispered. In her mind, she found her happy place: a beach, where her feet sank into the hot, white sand as she walked toward the aquiline water, the waves rolling onto the shore the only sound she could hear.

That and the voice of one Tommy Rowland, the hot-but-off-limits best friend of her new brother-in-law.

"Want me to grab you a piña colada?"

Yes. That's exactly what she'd be hearing.

She'd look over to see his tanned, muscled torso, his six-pack flexing as he walked, the sand sparkling in the trail of hair below his belly button. Before he headed back to the cocktail hut (because didn't every good beach have a cocktail hut?), she'd put her hands on his hips and pull him toward her, thanking him with a kiss.

And boy, was he a good kisser—at least, in her fantasy. Not that she'd know in real life. She groaned.

"Mom?"

Will's voice brought her out of her fantasy, dousing her (imagined) sun-kissed skin with a cold, wet dose of reality. She opened her eyes and cleared her throat.

"Weren't you both dressed at breakfast?"

They exchanged a look—the type of look that had become too common in the past year—and Wyatt made brief eye contact with her before looking at his feet. "We were, but the milk ... kind of ..." His throat worked and he looked up at her again just as his brother supplied the last word: "Exploded."

In Will's expression Pearl could see a sort of contained glee.

Don't cry over spilled milk.

The visualization exercise, which her therapist had recommended as an immediate stress reliever, wouldn't work now, not at the rate her throat constricted.

The only way the milk could have exploded was if—

"It's his fault." Wyatt elbowed his little brother, who elbowed him back. "What? It *is*, you big baby. You dropped it on the floor because your little muscles are too weak to hold it."

"It was *slippery*."

Sometimes Pearl wanted to run away. Not permanently, of course. But just for a few days. To get her sanity back. At the beach. She dragged in a breath, filling her lungs with plain oxygen rather than salty sea air. "I assume you're here in my bedroom because you want to tell me it's all cleaned up. Right?"

Despite the stress of the past week, as everything in the house broke down all at once, she had to laugh when they exchanged another look and scuttled back down the hallway, suddenly teammates rather than adversaries.

She called after them. "I know that when I come out, the milk is going to be cleaned up and you're going to be dressed and ready.

Because we have to leave in ten minutes and I don't want to be late for Aunt June."

That should do it. The boys never wanted to disappoint the other adults in their lives. Pearl experienced what was probably the millionth wave of gratitude for her sister's new family. Opal had married Cash Wilder, one of four brothers, and the entire Wilder clan had welcomed Pearl and her boys with open arms after her divorce from their dad.

For June, who was married to Cash's brother Sterling, the timing was right. She needed an assistant event planner as badly as Pearl—now a single mom—needed a job. The largest assisted living facility in Prescott had hired her to plan its Christmas party, which, according to June, had to be "dazzling, sparkling, magical ... and absolutely perfect."

Sure enough, when Pearl emerged from the bedroom a few minutes later, the boys were sitting side by side on the floor, tying their shoes.

"We put the towels in the washer." Wyatt tilted his head toward the kitchen.

Will jumped in before Pearl could respond to remind him that the washer was broken.

"But then we remembered the washer's broke, so we put them on the floor next to the washer."

Pearl forced a smile, stopped herself from correcting Will's use of "broke" and from lamenting the fact that they'd be dealing with sour-smelling towels later. "Great. Thanks, guys."

Thirty minutes later, she'd dropped off the boys. As soon as she waved them off (along with a reminder to behave and a threat that she'd better not receive any phone calls that day), she indulged herself and returned to her beach visualization.

"Now, where was I? Oh, yes. I was kissing Tommy Rowland." She'd end the kiss and give him a playful slap on the butt as he went back to the cocktail hut. Watching him go, she'd notice the way his swim trunks fit, hugging the curve of his ass. Because this was her fantasy, no one could judge her for the way she ogled him while he stood at the bar ordering their drinks. He'd turn around and wink at her, and then walk back to her, a drink in each hand, a little umbrella in each drink. He'd hand hers over, and they'd clink their glasses together.

Only, the clink sounded an awful lot like a pop. A pop that pulled Pearl out of her fantasy and filled her with very real dread in the very real world because it sounded exactly like a tire losing its air. Groaning, she pulled over. A quick roadside inspection revealed that her rear passenger side tire was, in fact, flat. The kind of flat where the rim sat right on the ground, squishing the rubber flat as a pancake.

"Perfect." Not only was she going to be late for work, but she was also going to have to get the tire repaired or—heaven forbid— replaced. She massaged her forehead with one hand, half-wishing the frigid air would kill her on the spot.

Leslie may not have been the best husband, but if he were here, he'd change the tire. He'd grumble and swear while he did it, but he'd do it. Groaning, she opened the trunk and started pulling out everything she'd jammed in there: camping chairs, the soccer wagon, soccer balls, an umbrella, a bag of potatoes she'd obviously missed when unloading groceries ...

A police car pulled up behind her, and her heart leapt. Maybe it was Tommy, coming to save the day. Despite the despair that had welled up, her lips twitched at that. Then she remembered he was taking a few weeks off work after an injury. So far, Cash had been mum about the details, which only piqued Pearl's curiosity.

The police car stopped and Pearl exhaled when she saw Cash getting out.

"It's just my luck to get to play hero to a beautiful woman on a freezing cold December morning." His drawl turned her lip twitching into an actual smile.

"Careful how you talk to me, or I'm going to tell my sister."

He waved a hand. "Ah, she'd be pleased as punch that I gave her sister a compliment."

She shrugged. "Probably true. As you can see, I've got a flat tire."

"That's real flat."

"I know. Goes along with my broken dishwasher and broken clothes washer."

He winced.

"And I've got half the house packed into the trunk."

"Including a bag of potatoes."

"Including a bag of potatoes." Suddenly, the situation didn't seem so bad. In fact, Pearl could see the humor in it.

"I assume you've got a spare in the trunk, and you're not unpacking half the house onto the highway because you've decided to live right here."

"You're correct. Although, that idea is appealing, some days."

"All right. Let me get that changed out for you, get you on your way. I assume you're headed to Sweet Springs to get with June on that big holiday to-do at the old folks' home." He moved to the trunk, lifted the panel, and started pulling out the tire.

"Yes. And I'm going to be late." Tears threatened and Cash must have heard the tightness in her throat because he said, "June's just about the sweetest girl I know, Pearl. She'll understand. It's not like anybody gets a flat tire on purpose."

He set the spare on the ground and pulled out the jack.

"I know, but it's just that I want so badly to be helpful to her. Not just because she's literally seconds from giving birth, but also because if this shindig goes well, she might keep me on permanently. And there's just so much I want to do for the boys, and it all costs money ... "

He was assembling the jack and glanced up at her near-hysteria, then flashed her the famous Wilder-brother-movie-star grin. "Pearl. You're doing great. Sterling said June's stress level has gone way down since you started helping her with the old folks' party." He breathed warm air onto his hands and rubbed them together before placing the jack.

"I think you should probably call it the Peaceful Pines party."

"Right. Peaceful Pines." Again, he grinned. "Plus, they're having a baby. I have a feeling June will do everything in her power to keep you on."

A fresh wave of emotion hit her—gratitude for his kindness. He started turning the handle to raise the jack.

"You think so?"

"I do. Now hand me that four-way wrench, will you?"

She did, and within a few minutes, he'd put on the spare tire, found a nail in the main tire, and helped her load everything back into the trunk.

"Now, get outta here. I think you've only lost about ten minutes. When you get to June's, you can blame me for being a slow tire changer."

Laughing now, she squeezed his arm and thanked him, and was on her way. Driving past the *Welcome to Sweet Springs Ranch* sign and up the tree-lined driveway always relaxed her. There was something about the country setting—away from the hustle and bustle of the small downtown—that let a soul *breathe*.

June came bustling out of the main house the moment Pearl parked, which sent her into full-fledged guilt mode again. She was already apologizing for being late, and June was already waving her off. "It's fine, I promise. Cash called Sterling and said you were having a rough morning and you being late is his fault because he's a slow tire changer."

Again, Pearl had to laugh. She loved this family and couldn't believe how lucky she was that she was part of it. "I'll also place some of the blame on my darling children, who exploded a gallon of milk this morning."

June wrinkled her nose. "Oh, boy."

"Yeah. This is what you have to look forward to. Although I'm sure your child will be a complete angel."

"I'm sure he won't. But that's okay."

"Well, I'm here now, so put me to work. What do you want me to do?"

June gestured to the little cottage where she kept her home office. "Come on in. I've updated the whiteboard with everything we have left to do. We'll just start knocking things out."

"How are you feeling today?" Pearl inclined her head toward June's rounded belly.

June sighed. "I hate to complain, really—I'm so excited about this baby. But I'm big and uncomfortable and my ankles are swollen and I can't sleep to save my life."

"I remember those days well. It's all going to be worth it."

Running a hand over her baby bump as they entered the office, June smiled. "I can't wait." She gasped and grabbed Pearl's wrist. "Ohmygod. Either I just peed my pants, or my water broke."

Panic swirled in. June's water couldn't break. Not now. She wasn't due for three more weeks and she had to spearhead the Peaceful Pines holiday party. She couldn't leave Pearl in charge of it. But Pearl didn't say any of those things, because she could see that June was panicking, too. Eyes wide, mouth in a grimace, she intensified the grip on Pearl's wrist.

"Ohmygod, Pearl. What do I do?"

Forcing calm, Pearl pried June's hand off and held it gently. "You take a deep breath, okay? First things first."

She demonstrated and June followed along, nodding, her eyes still wide. She sucked in a breath and let it out.

"Good. Another." She held eye contact while June obeyed. "Is your hospital bag packed?"

June shook her head. "No. It's not. I thought I had time."

"Is Sterling here?"

Another shake of the head. "He should be back any minute. He just ran to the hardware store."

"Okay. Let's go back to the house and pack your bag. If he's not back to take you to the hospital, I'll take you, get you checked in, and wait with you until he comes. Okay?"

Her nod was fast and jerky and she licked her lips. "Okay. Okay. I can do this."

"You can do this. Come on."

Sterling arrived just as they zipped the bag, and he wore an expression as wild-eyed as June's. Heart aching at the memory of going into labor with Wyatt, Pearl hugged them both. "You guys are going to do great. This time tomorrow, you'll have an adorable bundle of joy in your arms."

"But Pearl. The party. What are we going to do?"

Feigning confidence, Pearl smiled. "You focus on the baby. I'll focus on the party. We've both got this."

Then they were off, leaving Pearl on her own.

Chapter Two

Tommy Rowland couldn't believe his luck. It was terrible. Horrible. The worst. Sitting at home for the tenth day in a row, he stared down at what remained of his finger. His trigger finger, no less.

He should get off the couch and do something, but he just couldn't make himself. Although the TV was on, he paid it no attention.

For about the millionth time, his mind flashed to the memory of the moment that would change his life forever. A moment so much like so many other moments, he could scream.

Just like any other day, he was patrolling downtown when dispatch came on the radio reporting a car accident. Just like any other day, he was nearby and responded. Just like any other day, when he noticed a passenger still in the car's backseat, he opened the door—which was crushed from the impact—to help her out. The door was stuck, which wasn't unusual, so he used all his strength to pull it open. The passenger was able to climb out, and he released the door, which slammed shut—on his hand.

It hurt, but no more than many of the other injuries he'd suffered in his lifetime. The broken collarbone when he fell off a slide. The slashed-open thigh when he was whittling a butterfly for his junior high girlfriend. The broken ankle when he crashed his dirt bike sophomore year.

The angle was so awkward, he couldn't open the car door again, and had to use his radio to call for help. Cash Wilder showed up next, and only gave him a half-hearted ribbing for having his hand stuck in the door. They got it free and when Tommy looked it over, he figured it'd heal fast. Yes, it was bruised, and yes, it was bleeding, but hadn't he had about a million instances of bruised and bleeding?

Only, after a few days, it hadn't improved at all and Cash convinced him to go in for an x-ray. All the bones in his finger were obliterated. The doctor declared it inoperable, said it wouldn't heal on its own, and scheduled an amputation. Of his finger. Not just any finger, but his trigger finger.

On its own, the surgery meant taking six weeks off work (for a *finger* injury). But the fact that he was now missing his trigger finger? The only way he could go back to work was if he relearned shooting—with his middle finger or his left hand.

Both of which seemed absolutely ridiculous.

A Christmas commercial came on, all jingling music and twinkling lights, and he cursed and turned off the TV. What did he want with Christmas commercials? He couldn't get in the holiday spirit right now. He needed to focus on getting back to work.

He had six weeks, which was at once a blessing and a curse. He had plenty of time to practice his new shooting technique, but how long could a guy spend at the shooting range every day? Six weeks' worth of mostly empty days stretched ahead of him.

His phone rang, startling him. "Cash, my man." He infused his voice with as much cheer as he could.

"Tommy! Bro! How you doin'?" Road noise in the background told Tommy Cash was out and about.

Jealousy flared. He gritted his teeth. "Same old, same old."

"Listen."

Oh, God. Tommy braced himself. He'd heard so much advice from well-meaning friends and family lately. Pick up a book of crossword puzzles. Play that word game on your phone. Read a novel.

Cash went on. "You'll never guess who I just got to play hero for."

Intrigued, Tommy felt his shoulders relax. "Who?"

"Pearl Houston."

Tommy groaned. He let Cash think his reaction was a result of Cash's repeated attempts to get him to ask her out, but it was really a result of his own attraction to Pearl and his inability to do anything about it. "Yeah?"

"Yeah. She had a flat tire."

"You change it for her?"

"I did."

Another flare of jealousy, because she'd probably rewarded Cash with that smile that turned Tommy into mush. "What are you telling me for?"

"Oh! Right. She mentioned that her dishwasher and clothes washer are broken. At the same time."

"And?" More gritting of his teeth.

"And I thought, who better than you to go over there and help her out? You've got some time on your hands. Wait. Do we still call it a hand even though it's missing the most important finger?" A pause and then, "Wait. Too soon? Sorry, man. I'm just giving you shit. Anyway, I thought maybe you could go over there and do some, you know, repairs."

That final word sounded so dirty, Tommy had to laugh. "Repairs, huh?"

"Yeah. You know how to fix stuff, right?"

Tommy dropped his forehead into his hand. "Yeah. I know how to fix stuff."

"And you've got time on your hand."

"Screw you, bro."

Cash cackled. "But seriously."

"I'll think about it."

"What is there to think about? You got big plans for the day?"

"No, but—" *She probably doesn't want the village idiot at her house.* He cursed himself—again—for being stupid enough to damage his finger beyond repair.

"I know what you're thinking."

Restless, Tommy stood up. "Oh, yeah? What am I thinking?"

"You're thinking it's so stupid you have to take six weeks off work for a stupid finger injury, and Pearl and the boys are going to be grossed out by your missing finger."

"Close enough." He paced the living room.

"You don't have to tell the kids you smashed your finger, man. Closed the door on it, yourself. You can tell them something cool, like a dragon burned it off with his fire breath when you were saving the alien princess. Or, like, you cut it off with your lightsaber when you were saving the entire world from an evil cyborg bent on universal domination."

"I think you're mixing too many worlds here."

"Kids eat that shit up. Tell them whatever you want. They'll think it's cool."

"I don't know."

"You know what? You sound depressed, dude. How long's it been since you got out of the house?"

Still pacing, Tommy shrugged. "I don't know. Couple of days."

Ten days. Since he came home from the hospital, one finger short.

"Come over for dinner tonight."

"I can't."

"Got something going?"

"No, man. I just don't want to leave the house. Look, I appreciate the offer, but can I take you up on it some other time?"

"It's gotta be today."

Tommy laughed. "It does, huh?"

"Yeah. Today's the only day. I've got to go. I've got a call coming in. Be at our place at six, okay? I'm setting an extra place for you."

"You set places?"

"No. It's something I've heard people say. Just show up, okay?" He disconnected before Tommy could respond.

With a sigh so dramatic, he would have laughed at himself under any other circumstances, Tommy tossed his phone onto the couch and went in search of the gift Cash had bought him a few days before: a practice target. It connected to the sight on his gun and an app on his phone so he could practice his shooting at home.

Because he was so resentful of the need for it, he'd yet to set it up. But he figured now was as good a time as any. At least he'd have something to talk to Cash and Opal about at dinner ... other than his complete and utter boredom with sitting at home feeling sorry for himself.

He reached for the utility knife he always kept in his pocket and cursed (again) when he remembered he was still wearing the shorts he slept in, which didn't have pockets or even the structure to hold a knife. Once he found the knife on top of his dresser (along with everything he kept in his gun belt), he opened the target box and tossed the instructions aside.

The target itself was a thin piece of plastic, and it had spots for him to attach the feet so it could stand on a table. He downloaded the app on his phone and slid his phone into the spot on the target before retrieving his gun from the safe. He double checked that it wasn't loaded, and then affixed the laser beam on the muzzle.

Before he aimed, he tried using his middle finger to dry fire a few times. "Awkward as hell." Frustration filled his torso hot and fast and he forced himself to take a few deep breaths and try again. "Still awkward." *But better.*

He'd never be proficient with his middle finger. But, he had to get there, if he ever hoped to get back to the road. He lifted the gun, aimed at the abstract painting behind the couch, and pulled the trigger again. Even without the laser and target, he could see the wobble in his hand.

"Imagine retiring on disability for a smashed finger."

He shook his head, admonishing himself yet again. Then he made sure the target and app were all set up and took a few shots. He moved closer to look at his grouping and cringed. "Terrible."

He'd never have passed shooting in the academy if he was that bad. How would he get re-qualified now?

Out of nowhere, a memory hit him: little league, the year he was in fifth grade. He couldn't hit the ball to save his life. His coach ended the practice with a batting lineup, and he was last to go. Some kids hit their first pitch, and everyone hit the ball by their fifth or sixth swing. But not Tommy.

After the tenth pitch, the coach had another kid round up all the balls behind the plate so he could pitch some more. One by one, his teammates' parents started taking them home, and before long, it was just the coach and his own kid and Tommy, whose dad stood by third base, arms crossed.

After the twentieth or maybe fortieth pitch, Tommy started to get frustrated. The coach must have been able to see it, because he said, "Son, relax. You're never gonna hit the thing if you're all tensed up. I'll pitch to you a hundred times if I have to. A thousand. Once you get it, you'll have it. But you won't get it if you're all wound up."

Tommy glanced at his dad, who simply nodded, encouraging him. The coach must have pitched to him a hundred more times. And sure enough, he hit the ball eventually. And then he hit another and another.

On the way home that night, his dad said something like, "Good man, that Coach Barrett. Good man."

By the end of the season, Tommy's teammates were calling him Slugger and high-fiving him when he hit home runs.

Feeling somewhat bolstered, all-grown-up Tommy ran through Coach Barrett's pep talk again, calmed himself down, and aimed his gun. His grouping was still terrible, but he might just have to pull that trigger a hundred times. Or a thousand.

Chapter Three

The events of Pearl's day served only to prove to her that the weeks leading up to the Peaceful Pines holiday party were going to be complete chaos. After seeing June and Sterling off, she'd commandeered June's office and whiteboard and determined that she was going to be on the run from sun-up until sundown for ... well, for the rest of her life, roughly.

It was five p.m. and she sat at the desk in June's office, her head in her hands. Christmas music played on the Bluetooth speaker, all merry and bright and jingling bells, and she hoped the speaker could hear the irritation in her voice when she told it to stop playing.

She'd put it on first thing, hoping the music would keep her focused and in the mood. But now, after an entire day, she yearned for some screaming hard rock.

About noon, she texted June for an update, and learned that June was still in the early stages of labor and was feeling fine.

Around two, she realized she'd have to leave in forty-five minutes to pick up the boys and texted Opal, begging her to pick them up, narrowly avoiding a breakdown. When Opal texted an hour later insisting Pearl come to dinner, Pearl nearly wept with relief.

By five, she'd determined that she was definitely going to have to bring some work home with her, so she stopped rubbing her forehead and forced herself to focus on what, exactly, that was.

The snowflakes. Those were something she could do at home. She found the package of approximately one million paper snowflakes and put it in a crate. The playlist. June told her a generic holiday playlist wasn't good enough; she (June) had promised the Pleasant Pines director, Marge Esperanza, that she'd handpick every single song.

"It's how you make people feel special—you handpick as much as you can," she'd said, back in the days when they'd both assumed they'd be working together right up until the holiday party.

Pearl found the handwritten list June had started and set it in the crate, too.

"The centerpieces!" She could assemble those at home, too. Into the crate they went.

Finally, she added the notebook in which she'd written down the information from the handyman—information that basically told her she'd never afford Christmas gifts for the boys this year.

She locked up the office, the cold stinging her cheeks so that she rushed to her car, where she was shocked to see the time on the dashboard: 6:00.

"Already?" Her voice came out in a wail, and she gave herself permission to wallow for exactly as long as it took her to get to Opal and Cash's house. Then she'd put on a brave face for the boys. After firing off a quick text to June (*I won't bug you again but just wanted you to know I'm thinking of you*), she headed for her sister's.

The first thing she noticed when she reached the front door: silence. Which meant her children were dead—she shook her head at her own humor—or sitting in front of electronics in some form. Not wanting to disrupt the blessed silence, she went in without knocking.

And there, in the middle of the living room, stood her six-year-old first grader, a gun in his hands.

Pearl gasped and froze, her mind racing. The boys were experienced with guns, and Cash had asked if he could work with them on target practice, but why did Will have a gun *now*? She moved toward Will as quickly as she could. His head whipped toward her, his arms following the movement. Just as she noticed the orange tip on the (fake) gun, a voice from inside the living room said, "Second rule of gun safety?"

Again, Pearl froze.

Like a robot, Will dropped his arms so the gun pointed at the floor. "Never point the gun at something you don't want to destroy."

"Right."

"Even though it's not a real gun." Will's voice was matter-of-fact, like they'd gone over that rule several times.

Inhaling deeply in hopes of hiding her momentary panic, Pearl made calm, measured strides toward the living room. There, in a line along the wall, stood Opal, Cash, Wyatt and ... and Tommy Rowland.

If she hadn't been so caught up in her son holding a firearm (a fake one, but still, it had looked so *real*), she would have swooned. Tommy was always good-looking, but when a person wasn't expecting him, his looks were disarming. Disorienting. Heart-stopping.

And that was before he smiled.

It was as if the floor went out from under Pearl and she felt herself smiling back, dazed, all the stress of the day melting right out of her tense shoulders, that spot between her eyebrows, even the tiny muscle in her temple that she didn't notice until she'd developed a migraine. All that tension—gone.

"Hi, Pearl." From the exaggerated way he enunciated her name, it was obvious that he either wasn't expecting her or that he'd caught her reacting to him like a deer in headlights.

Oh, God. "Hi, Tommy."

At the edge of her consciousness, she registered Opal and Cash exchanging a look as exaggerated as Tommy's greeting, and then they both said, "Hi, Pearl."

"Mommy!" Will spun toward her, the gun still trapped in his fist and pointed at the floor. "Tommy's teaching us to shoot."

"Yeah!" Wyatt ran up to her and grabbed her hands. "He's letting us use his dummy gun." His eyes went round even while he smiled at the word dummy, and she thought she hadn't seen the boys lit up like this since the divorce.

Tommy cleared his throat. "I, uh—I feel like I should interject, here."

She had no choice but to look at him, to make eye contact—something she usually avoided because of how it made her feel. Like *this*. Like she never wanted to look away. She couldn't form any coherent thoughts, much less words. Fortunately, he kept talking, his hands resting against his stomach.

"I didn't know you—well, you and the the kids—were going to be here." He threw a dark look at Cash, who shrugged, his infamous devilish grin flashing. "Cash bought me this—" he paused, cleared his throat. "He bought me this target." He held up his hand to point at the rectangular piece of plastic standing on the fireplace surround, and that's when Pearl noticed. He wasn't actually pointing, because his pointer finger was gone. He seemed to notice, too, and made a frustrated sound deep in his throat before hooking his thumb at the target, instead.

Pearl glanced at the boys and saw them looking somberly at Tommy's hand.

"I was using it before I came over here and I wanted to show it to Cash. So I brought it with me. We were using it when Opal brought the boys in and—"

"And we *begged* him to try it." Wyatt supplied the rest of the explanation, and then Will jumped in, too. "But don't worry, Mama. Mr. Tommy taught us the rules of gun safety before he even let us touch his gun. Even though it's not a real gun."

And right then, out of nowhere, Pearl had an image of the most vixen-like version of herself asking Tommy if he could teach her the rules of gun safety so she could use his gun. She swore her face turned thirty shades of red and Opal must have known exactly what she was thinking because she grinned. "What are the rules of gun safety, you little sharpshooters?"

"The gun is always loaded." Wyatt glanced at Tommy, who gave him a thumbs up.

"Never point the gun at something you don't want to destroy."

Will growled out the last word, making Cash and Opal laugh. Tommy's eyes twinkled, but he gave Will a serious thumbs up, too. "Keep your finger off the trigger 'til you're ready to shoot."

"Will! It's my turn."

Pearl inhaled to interject, but Tommy spoke first. "Now you do two, Wyatt."

Smug, Wyatt nodded. "Know your target and what's behind it. And ... oh, yeah! Know how to use your gun."

"Good job, bud. And the last one is to store your gun safely. Which is why I'll be locking it in its safe while we eat dinner."

"Even though it's not a real gun," Will said again.

"Right. Just for safety," Tommy said.

"Which is what we're going to do right now," Opal said. "Why don't you give the gun back to Mr. Tommy, Will, and you guys can set the table."

Opal and Cash made themselves scarce.

"Remember what I showed you," Tommy told Will, who somehow managed to hand the gun to Tommy without pointing it at him. "Good job, man. I'll put it away now."

"Thanks for letting us use your gun," Wyatt said, and Will said, "Yeah, thanks for letting us *shoot* stuff!"

Opal called for the boys and those two deserted Pearl without a second thought, leaving her alone with Tommy. Only then did she notice the Christmas tree in the corner, and quite unexpectedly, she burst into tears.

Tommy, who was taking his gun apart, paused and looked at her, and his obvious uncertainty about how to handle the situation—how to handle *her*—made her laugh even while she cried. "Don't worry. I'm fine. Keep doing your gun thing."

He nodded and looked away, placing the gun into the safe that sat next to the target. She sniffled, dug into her pockets for tissue, and came up empty. "I'm really sorry. I'll be right back."

In the bathroom, she blew her nose as quietly as she possibly could, then used one of Opal's washcloths to dab some cold water under her eyes. When she reemerged, she found Tommy still sitting on the fireplace surround, hands in his lap. The idea that he might be waiting for her at once mortified and pleased her.

"You okay?"

She nodded. "Yeah. I'm really sorry. It's been a long day. A long week, actually. And I just realized how close to Christmas it is, and I haven't even gotten a tree for the boys."

"We could steal this one." His eyes were soft with kindness and sparkling with mischief.

For the first time that day, she felt a genuine smile form on her lips. "Great idea. Pretend to leave after dinner, wait outside until Opal and Cash turn off the lights, and then sneak back in and whisk it away. They'll never know."

"Exactly my thoughts. We'd make excellent partners in crime." His gaze shifted to focus on something behind Pearl, and she turned around to see Opal's head sticking out from behind the wall that separated the living room from the kitchen. Spying.

"Ready for dinner?" She was all innocence, but Pearl knew she'd been hoping to catch the two of them in a flirtatious conversation. *Had she?*

Naturally, the only two seats remaining at the table were side by side, which, Pearl suspected, was by design. Opal avoiding eye contact only confirmed that suspicion. She was still deciding whether to be annoyed or amused when Tommy pulled out her chair for her. Amused, for sure.

"Thank you." She gave him a weird little curtsy-head-bob thing she wished she could delete.

He smiled at her. She smiled back. Opal and Cash exchanged yet another look. *I'm definitely going to have to avoid family dinners after this.*

Chapter Four

Tommy was certain his death certificate would list boredom as the cause of his demise. The morning after dinner with Pearl (well, Opal, Cash, and Pearl's boys, too), he dragged himself out of bed at eight (the earliest he'd done since the surgery). He drank coffee, scrolled through the news, and brushed his teeth. That was all he had on the agenda. Which was why he'd been sleeping so late.

At nine, he sat at his dining room table, staring at what remained of his right pointer finger.

He'd known he couldn't avoid people seeing it forever, but even now, he could literally feel his skin crawling with the shame of Pearl noticing it the night before. As huge as that moment felt to him, it seemed but a blip on her radar—she'd mentioned a long day and her expression was tense most of the evening.

Except when he'd joked about stealing the Christmas tree. Then her face had relaxed and she'd given him a genuine smile and he knew then and there he'd do anything to see that smile again. His mind replayed that moment over and over in slow motion, and he let his imagination change it up.

His phone rang and Cash's name came up on the screen.

"Hey, man. Don't you have anything better to do on your day off than to call me?"

His friend's laugh was infectious. "I do—a honey-do list about a mile long. Opal's got these new goats coming in—"

"I thought she was starting a horse and dog rescue." Tommy drummed his fingers on the tabletop and stopped when he noticed his missing finger threw off the rhythm.

"Yeah, well, I guess you could say it's morphed. The people who she fostered those puppies for last year? They called and said they have a handful of goats that need fostering. They knew she had the horses and the property, so—"

"So now you're building a goat enclosure."

"Right."

"Are you calling for help?" Hope flickered in Tommy's chest. In the days since his surgery, everybody told him he should be taking things easy. He figured the guys were going out for drinks after their shift, or for a game of pool on the weekend nights. But nobody invited him. He supposed he could invite himself, but that was just too awkward.

"In a way."

The little flicker of hope wobbled. "What do you mean?"

"Here's the thing. It's my day off, as you know."

"Right."

"And, as you know, Pearl's dishwasher and clothes washer broke."

"You told me yesterday. And when I saw her at your house, she mentioned she had a long day."

"Yeah, from what the boys said, it also involved an exploded gallon of milk. And June going into labor. Still hasn't had the baby, by the way, but what it means for Pearl is that she's on her own for this holiday party thing for the old folks' home."

"Which you should probably stop calling it."

"Right. Peaceful Pines."

"So you called me ..."

"Right. I called you to see if you could be a dear and go over to Pearl's, take a look at her appliances."

"Bro."

"I know. I couldn't resist."

"I told you yesterday, I can't do it."

"Can't check out her appliances?"

Tommy groaned. Again.

"Just go over and see what you can do. Maybe a little plumbing?"

Pacing now, Tommy said, "You just can't get enough of this, can you?"

"What?"

"'What?' Like you're all innocent. I'll go check out her appliances, but don't think you're doing any matchmaking, Wilder."

"My intentions are pure, bro. Lady needs some help. You're bored out of your mind. I know you were just sitting around, agonizing over your stupid finger."

Tommy grunted.

"And as for the matchmaking accusation, why ever not, Rowland?"

At that, he spluttered. "Because."

"*So* not a reason."

"Because, bro. She's recently divorced. I'm fingerless. What does a woman want with a fingerless man?"

"She's been divorced for more than a year. Remember? She had the kids on her own at Halloween last year, and it's almost Christmas. *And*, you're not even fingerless. You've got seven other fingers and two thumbs. There's plenty you can do with all that. Plus, I'm getting a literal contact high from the chemistry between you two."

Tommy sighed, and made sure to make his exhale extra loud, so Cash could hear it over the phone.

"Besides. All I'm asking is for a favor to me. I told Pearl I'd help her today and I've got to get these goat pens built. I could do all of it, because I'm so amazing, but like I said, you've got nothing going. Plus, she's not even going to be there. She's at Sterling and June's, working in the office."

Huh. That bit of news was as much of a relief as it was a disappointment. But if she wasn't going to be there, all he had to do was figure out what was wrong with the appliances and, hopefully, fix them. The idea of fixing something for Pearl was appealing. Beyond appealing. "All right."

"You'll do it?"

"Yeah. I'll do it. But you said she's not going to be home, right?"

"Right. I mean, she might have to meet you there to let you in and give you her key. Because Opal and I are going to the hardware store."

"Doesn't Opal have a key? You guys could just meet me while you're out."

"Nope. Sorry, man. I'll text Pearl and have her meet you in an hour. Okay?"

Bamboozled again. He had no choice but to agree, so he did. And so what if he changed his shirt and sprayed on some cologne before he walked out the door?

He got to her house before she did, and considered driving around the block a couple of times so he wouldn't appear too anxious. Before he could decide, she pulled into the driveway next to him.

"I'm so sorry." Her greeting removed any concern over what to say first, and she didn't leave space for him to respond before she went on. "I told Cash not to bother you, that we could wait. The boys need to learn to hand wash dishes anyway, and I can go to the laundromat."

While she talked, he took in her appearance. She wore dark jeans and a dusky blue sweater that perfectly matched the color of her eyes. The cold made her cheeks pink, and he imagined kissing her in the falling snow.

"You didn't have to come, but Cash said you were bored and didn't mind, and I really don't want to supervise hand washing or go to the laundromat. I'll pay you."

"I won't accept payment. Consider it a favor to a friend."

She wrinkled her nose in the most adorable way. "I have to do something. I'll find a way to make it up to you, okay?"

Let me think of all the ways. "Okay." He nodded, business-like. "But let me look at the stuff, first. If I can't fix them, or if I make things worse, which is a possibility, then you might change your tune."

There was that laugh again—the same one he'd heard when he suggested stealing Cash and Opal's Christmas tree. God, he'd pay every cent in his possession to hear it.

"Let me show you the kitchen and laundry room, and then I'll get out of your hair. I've got a huge task list for this holiday party."

Inside, Tommy noticed right away that Pearl's broken appliances were resulting in chaos. On the counters, clean dishes sat on laid-out dish towels. Towers of dirty dishes were stacked in the sink. A glance into the dining room revealed similarly large piles of laundry stuffed into hampers.

"I feel like I should apologize for the mess." Pearl's shoulders slumped as she looked around the space.

"It's fine. I know how fast these things stack up."

"They do. I mean, we've been doing our best to keep up, but our best isn't good enough, as you can see. Anyway, here's the dishwasher. It's just not cleaning the dishes. And there's the laundry room. The washer is leaking. I can't even tell where the water's coming from." Her movements looked defeated, like exhaustion overpowered her ability to do any more than lift an arm toward each broken appliance.

"I want to tell you we'll get your appliances up and running in no time, but I don't want to overpromise." He grimaced, and she smiled and grabbed his hand.

The gesture was innocent enough, friendly. But the contact? Not innocent at all. Feeling her skin, soft against his palm, made him want to feel it all over his body. And then she dropped his hand. The intense desire remained.

"No pressure. I can't tell you how much I appreciate you looking at them."

Their phones dinged at the same time, and after glancing at each other, they looked at their screens. Pearl squealed. "The baby's here! Opal just texted! Look at him!"

She showed the picture to Tommy, whose heart swelled, not

only at the baby's newborn scowl, but also at Pearl's reaction. "Cash texted me, too! That's a good-lookin' baby."

Misty-eyed, Pearl looked at the picture again. "In a few short years, he'll be leaving his socks on the living room floor and bickering over whose turn it is to take out the trash."

Tommy laughed. "You don't even want to think about what they'll all be doing during their teenage years."

Pearl covered her ears. "Don't tell me." Then she looked at the photo again. "Aw, he's just the cutest. I'm so happy for them."

"Me, too," Tommy said. "But I'm still sorry his arrival means you're on your own for the holiday party."

"I'll be fine. June said I can consult with her if I need to, but I don't want to bug her. Anyway, having my dishwasher and clothes washer back will really help. I don't know if Cash told you, but the guy I called wanted to charge me seven-fifty to repair them."

"*Seven hundred and fifty?*" Tommy whistled, long and low. "That's insane."

"I know. Right before Christmas. Can you believe it?"

"I mean, a guy has to make a living, but surely it's not going to take that long to fix these." *I hope.*

"That's what I thought. But what do I know? I'm a brand new assistant event planner with absolutely no experience in repairing appliances. Fake swords? Yes. Broken shinguards? Check. Nerf guns? Sure. But not the machinery that runs our lives."

"Let me see what I can do."

She nodded. "Okay. Again, thank you so much. And good luck. Obviously, I'll pay you for anything you need to buy. Parts, tools, gas, anything. You know what? Let's exchange numbers and that way you can text me and I'll send you money."

Tommy's inner teenage boy did a fist pump as he gave her his number and she texted him, *Hi,* with a smiley-face emoji. After one more thank you, she left and he was alone in her house, doing his very best to focus on appliances rather than trying to pick up Pearl-related clues from her photos, furniture, and decorations.

He felt like a sponge, desperate to soak her in. "And now I'm getting poetic."

A handful of YouTube videos later, he felt somewhat confident about investigating the dishwasher's problem. He hit pay dirt on the first thing he checked: the filter was completely clogged. It was entirely possible one of the boys had emptied a bowl of actual dirt right into the bottom of the machine. The internet offered plenty of advice on cleaning a clogged filter, so he followed what seemed like the most thorough instructions and then loaded the dishwasher for a trial run.

Then he moved onto the clothes washer, which proved a little more complicated. Upon initial inspection, he found that filter was a little clogged, too, but not so badly it should cause a leak. After a few minutes of hunting around, he found the problem: one of the fittings that connected the wall spigot to the hose was cracked, so whenever the machine ran, it spewed water down the wall and onto the floor.

He'd have to replace the fitting and the hose, but he had no idea where to buy washer parts. Yet another scouring of the Internet revealed the hardware store didn't carry any. He'd have to call a local appliance store. When the woman who answered the phone confirmed she had the parts, he walked out to his truck with a spring in his step.

This was the first time in days that he'd moved with a sense of purpose, and it felt damn good.

Chapter Five

Who could blame a girl for daydreaming about a man like Tommy Rowland, envisioning him in her house, his muscles flexing as he worked on her appliances? That's exactly what Pearl did, beginning immediately after leaving him in her kitchen, and ending only when her phone rang during the last hour of the school day and she saw the school's phone number on the screen.

"What now?" Her whisper-groan echoed against the walls of the quiet office.

A glance at the clock told her Wyatt's teacher was on her break. The kids were in music class. Only someone who received many, many calls from her child's teacher would know the schedule so intimately, she thought as she tapped the screen to answer.

"Mrs. Marshall?"

Pearl cleared her throat and said for the zillionth time, "It's Ms. Houston now. Wyatt's mom."

"Oh!" Mrs. Gutierrez's voice went up a couple of octaves. "Of course. I'm sorry. Yes. Ms. Houston. I'm calling about Wyatt?"

It took all of her willpower to suppress a groan. "Again."

A tinkling sound came through her earpiece—the laughter was

so unexpected, she didn't recognize it at first. "Based on our history, I can see why you thought I was calling about something negative."

"You're not?" Pearl's hackles relaxed the tiniest bit.

"No. I'm calling, Ms. Houston, because your son did the sweetest thing today. There's a new student in our class whose family has been struggling. He hasn't been bringing a lunch and was too embarrassed to ask the cafeteria staff for food. Well today, I happened to be walking through the cafeteria and there's the new student with a huge pile of food in front of him. I'm talking sandwiches, fruit, chips, juice boxes ... you name it, he had it. Wyatt was sitting next to him, so I called Wyatt over and asked him where the student had gotten all that food. He wouldn't say."

Mrs. Gutierrez had probably thought Wyatt was being obstinate, per usual.

"I thought he was just being stubborn. So I called another kid over and eventually, I put together the pieces to discover that Wyatt spearheaded a little food bank for this kid. He got all his friends together and everybody chose one thing to double up on in their lunch boxes. They fed this kid, and they have plans to keep right on doing it."

Tears sprang to Pearl's eyes. With everything they'd been through since the divorce—and Wyatt's subsequent behavior—she was literally overjoyed that he'd been so thoughtful. And not just that, but he put his thoughtfulness into action. "Wow." The single word was all she could manage.

"I know." Ms. Gutierrez chuckled. "Turns out, Wyatt was reluctant to tell me what was going on because he didn't want the adults to stop the kids from bringing food for their new classmate."

"That's so sweet." Her whisper sounded strangled. "What great kids."

"Great kids. And now that we know what's going on, we're going to make sure the new student gets breakfast and lunch at school. But I just wanted to share something positive. I know it's been a rough year."

Boy, has it. "Thank you, Ms. Gutierrez. I really appreciate it."

"You're welcome. Thank you for raising an amazing young man."

They disconnected and Pearl burst into tears. What a *relief*. Maybe she was doing something right after all. Maybe the divorce and the subsequent co-parenting and two households and separate holidays wouldn't actually ruin her children's chances at turning out okay.

When Wyatt got in the car twenty minutes later, she felt herself getting all teary again, and had to pull yet another tissue from the box she'd grabbed at the office.

"What's wrong?" Wyatt's eyebrows knitted together as he slid across the backseat.

"I'm just so proud of you." Her voice wavered. "Ms. Gutierrez called today and told me what you did for that other kid. That was so nice, Wyatt. I couldn't ask for anything more."

He blinked. "So, you're not gonna be mad that I got an F on my math test?"

"I mean..." she shrugged. "Not right now. But we'd better sit down and look at what you're missing, okay?"

"Okay."

"You got an F?" Will climbed into the car just in time to hear the end of the conversation, and Wyatt answered in typical fashion: "Sure did. What's it to you, dummy?"

Pearl sighed, rolled her eyes, and second-guessed her decision to celebrate Wyatt's kindness by taking them to the park and then out to an early dinner.

But, she didn't want to cook, she didn't know if the dishwasher was fixed, and she didn't want to go home to the house, which bore too many reminders that her life was currently pandemonium. She pictured the laundry piles on the couch and in the laundry room, and the dishes covering every square inch of flat space in the kitchen. And she decided that she'd give them all a break.

The boys cheered when she announced her plan, and the three of them laughed and talked through dinner and ice cream. Just as she was scooping the last bite of ice cream out of her bowl and thinking she hadn't heard from Tommy—and trying to decide whether that implied good news or bad—he sent her a text: *All done. Heading home. I left your key in the inchworm. Cute little guy.* Had he been there all day? Her stomach churned at the thought. She'd expected him to spend maybe an hour or two, but the entire day? She'd never be able to repay him. Maybe he'd finished earlier and forgotten to text. But if he had stayed all day, then maybe he'd gotten a lot done.

As desperate as she was for more information, Pearl wrote back, *Great! Thank you!* and left it at that. Pumping him for details wouldn't do. She'd feel pushy and unappreciative.

The short conversation reminded her that the evening was nothing but a temporary reprieve. Her shoulders and neck tensed as she closed the distance to home. The inchworm waited next to the front door and her house key tumbled out when she turned the statue upside down.

The boys were full of questions about why the key was in the inchworm and who'd been at their house and whether a robber could be inside, but the moment Pearl unlocked the door, she was speechless and incapable of answering.

The kitchen was spotless. Not a single dish sat on the counter. The sink, empty, sparkled. She took a few more steps and realized that the laundry sitting on the couch was now folded. The hampers in the laundry room were empty.

"Holy cow," Wyatt said, drawing out the phrase. "Did, like, the dish and laundry fairy come over, or something?"

"What the heck?" Will said, breaking into a run to do laps around the living room. "It's so *clean* in here!"

And it was. Spotless. Cleaner than it had been in weeks.

Pearl's throat tightened yet again, and she cursed her fragile emotional state. Then shame set in, making her face hot. Her house was such a wreck, Tommy felt obligated to clean it. They'd been acquaintances for years, but they certainly weren't on clean-each-other's-houses terms.

"Who did this?" Wyatt wanted to know.

"Prob'ly Aunt Opal." Will nodded, sage.

"Was it Aunt Opal, Mom?"

She opened her mouth and croaked. "Um, I'm not sure. Let me text her. You guys go get your pajamas on."

The boys shocked her by running off to their bedrooms and she texted her sister, whose response came through right away: *Nope. Wasn't me. I'm knee-deep in goats over here. It was probably Tommy.* She added a heart-eyed emoji. *Anyway, the goats are so cute. You should bring the boys over to see them.*

Half a second later, another text came through: *OMG that is sooo cute if Tommy did your dishes and folded laundry. Wait. Did he fold *your* laundry? Don't tell me he folded your panties, Pearl Houston.*

Wait. Did he?

Phone in hand, she rushed over to the couch to check, and slumped with relief when she saw that he'd folded only the boys' clothes. She sank onto the couch. *He only folded the boys'.*

Opal wrote back with a smiling devil emoji. *Think he stole a pair of your undies to take home?*

Pearl: *Stop it.*

Opal: *Can't. Sorry. This is just too good. How are you gonna repay him? Not that you have to, and I'm sure he doesn't expect it. But I know you're going to feel obligated.*

Her sister had the audacity to add peach and eggplant emojis, and then another smiling devil.

"Mom?" Will emerged from the hallway, wearing his monster truck pajama top and his police car bottoms. Pearl set her phone aside, mostly because Opal was right—she did feel obligated to repay Tommy somehow.

"Yeah?"

Will looked expectant. "Was it Aunt Opal?"

She sighed. "No. It was Mr. Tommy."

"Mr. Tommy?" Now he looked uncertain. "He did all this?" He made a circle with his pointer finger.

Wyatt, overhearing only the last part of the conversation, jumped onto the couch next to Pearl, laughing out loud, clutching his stomach. "I can't believe Mr. Tommy folded our laundry and did our dishes! He's a *guy*."

"Wyatt Marshall. Just for that comment, you're going to be doing all the dishes and laundry for the next week. And you're lucky —it appears that guy also repaired both of our machines today so you won't have to do everything by hand."

That stopped his laughter. "Are you serious?"

"*So* serious."

"You can't do that!"

"I can. And I will. *Guys* can help out with chores, too. Anyway. It's bedtime. Let's go."

As she went through the routine with the boys—the brushing of teeth, the reading of stories, and the choosing of the next day's outfits—she thought over what she'd say to Tommy. She'd needed to thank him, of course, but she also needed to make it clear that aside from big repairs that she planned to pay him for, she didn't need or expect household help.

Chapter Six

Tommy figured someone should make doctors' waiting rooms more interesting. That way, his mind would be occupied and it would stop drifting to Pearl Houston.

Pearl Houston, who'd texted him the night before with a message that bordered on peeved. At first, it caught him off guard. He'd expected glowing gratitude, not prickly independence.

Thank you for repairing my appliances. I know the house was a mess, but you didn't have to fold clothes and wash dishes. We would have gotten caught up.

No emojis, no offers of dinner or beer, no effusive praise.

He wrote back, *You're welcome. And I know. Just trying to be helpful.*

Without responding to that, she answered, *You never told me how much money to send you.*

He took a page from her book and didn't respond.

He should have been totally put off by her apparent lack of gratitude. She obviously wasn't pleased with his going above and beyond, and shouldn't she be? But in her message, he could read her determination, her need for autonomy. And *that* turned him on.

"Tommy Rowland?" The surgeon's nurse was at the door, waiting for him to get up and follow her to the exam room. Her raised eyebrows suggested that wasn't the first time she'd called his name.

He jumped to his feet. Fortunately, the surgeon, Dr. Rodney, didn't make him wait too much longer before coming into the exam room. "How's the hand?"

Tommy held it up for inspection. "Fine. Good as new. Well, minus the one finger."

"You gone shooting yet?"

"Not with a loaded gun. My friend got me this electronic target to practice dry firing at home, but I haven't gone to the range yet."

"I'd feel better clearing you to go back to work if you'd gone to the range, run a magazine through a gun." His smile was kind, his eyes warm.

Still, anger was all Tommy could feel. His molars ground together and he relaxed his jaw muscles before speaking. "I know. I'll go." He couldn't admit to another man that he was scared. Scared to go alone. Scared to go with someone else and fail. Scared he'd never be able to fire properly and would end up riding a desk for the rest of his career.

"Can I see the site?"

When Tommy nodded and held out his hand, Dr. Rodney began unwrapping it. Nausea set in and Tommy's gaze zoomed over to the poster on the wall.

Dr. Rodney's hands were cool and dry as he grasped Tommy's. "Looks great. No signs of infection. It's healing nicely."

Tommy wanted to ask him to wrap it up as quickly as possible, but he said, "Go ahead and leave it unwrapped now. Oxygen will do it a world of good.

Leave it unwrapped? Another, stronger wave of nausea hit him and his mouth watered. He swallowed, nodded.

"Listen, son. You're not the first strapping, good-looking young man to have to leave a wound unwrapped. Baring that scar can be a bit like baring your soul, whether it's your finger or your leg. But you're going to have to do it eventually, especially if you plan to go back to work. Bite the bullet, as they say, and you'll get used to it sooner rather than later. Fortunately, you've got that nice mug to distract people from it." He grinned. "Not my words. I heard some of the girls talking in the office." Squeezing Tommy's shoulder, he added, "I'll see you in five weeks. If you've put a bunch of rounds through your gun by then and you feel comfortable with it, I'll clear you to go back to work."

By the time he got back to his car, he had a text waiting from Cash: *Is your appointment over yet?*

As he typed up a quick recap, Tommy's shoulders started to relax. Waiting to clear him until he'd practiced shooting only made sense. In fact, hadn't he and Cash gotten into a situation just last year where they thought they might need their guns? He'd had a few more scares since. He'd feel like a real idiot if he wasn't sure whether he could shoot if he needed to.

He wrote back to Cash: *Yep. Doctor says I need to practice shooting real rounds before he'll clear me. Want to hit the range sometime in the next week?*

Cash replied right away with an emoji Tommy thought meant something like, *Rock on,* and then, *It's my day off, bro. Let me make sure Opal's not counting on my mad building skillz today, but if not, let's go!*

An hour later, they met at the police department's shooting range and in typical Cash fashion, he started talking as soon as they were both out of their vehicles, erasing any nerves Tommy might have thought he had.

"I have to say, I'm glad you're getting me out of the house, man." He grabbed his bag out of the bed of his truck and Tommy did the same. "Opal wanted to do a photo shoot with this group of goats. Let's just say it involved dressing them up."

Tommy shook his head. "I'm surprised you didn't stay. You seem pretty enthusiastic about all the other animal projects."

Cash laughed out loud as they walked up to the double doors. "I am, bro. But goat pictures?"

Tommy opened the door and the warm air rushed out to greet them. "What's she doing with them? Are they just for fun, or ..."

"To be fair, she plans to use them to help find homes for the goats. 'Imagine how cute they'll look in Christmas sweaters, Cash!

No one will be able to resist them!'" By now, they were laying out their guns and magazines and ammo and Tommy briefly registered their actions before Cash went on. "Maybe she's right, too. People love seeing animals dressed up. Especially at Christmas time. So maybe their little Santa hats and ugly sweaters *will* work."

Now they were loading their magazines, the motions as automatic as breathing—well, almost. They would be slightly more automatic if Tommy wasn't missing one of his most important fingers.

"Anyway, just so you know, I did tell her I'd stay and help if she wanted me to. That you and I could shoot this afternoon. But she insisted I come here."

"I'll be sure to thank her."

"Unless I humiliate you with my superior skill."

A flicker of uncertainty passed through Tommy's consciousness, but he forced it away. "I've always been able to beat you in a shootout, Wilder. Don't think anything's changed."

"Oh, we'll see, Rowland. Maybe I'll finally get my chance at a tighter group than you."

Getting into the rhythm now, they pressed the buttons to call back the targets and clipped on fresh ones. As the targets whizzed back out on their clotheslines, Tommy said, "Maybe I'll take a goat."

"I'm putting on my ear protection. That's a crazy idea."

Tommy put on his ear protection, too, and they both raised their weapons. He couldn't believe it. They'd gotten all the way to the point of actually shooting, and he hadn't had time for nerves.

"Last one to empty his magazine buys the beer."

Tommy's mouth dropped open and he scrambled for a response, an excuse, but Cash didn't even look at him—he just started shooting.

"I win that one. First round's on you. Let me reload and then you can try again."

By the end of ten turns, Tommy had caught up. His groupings weren't as tight as he'd like, but pulling the trigger with his middle finger felt somewhat natural. After each turn, they'd call back their targets, examine them, and then replace them with fresh ones, with barely a word.

Tommy had been so worried about Cash judging him, and about him judging himself, but they didn't leave enough time for that and now he felt foolish for anguishing over it.

"I'd say that's a wrap," Cash said as they cleaned up. "Not half-bad, Rowland."

"Sheesh, that's a real compliment coming from you."

"Take what you can get." Cash pulled his phone out of his back pocket and whistled. "Oh, boy. Looks like I'm about to have my hands full. Opal can't get the goats to look at the camera and one of them is trying to eat another one's sweater."

"But she's bound and determined to get these pictures taken, right?"

Cash grinned. "You know her well." His phone rang and he held it up so Tommy could see Opal's name on the screen. He answered. "Speak of the devil."

While he listened, he cringed, which piqued Tommy's curiosity. Then he walked away, talking low so Tommy couldn't hear him. Certainly he wouldn't be so secretive about the goat photo shoot. Tommy strained to hear, but couldn't. Eventually, Cash walked back, hung up and said, "Looks like you're going to have your hands full, too."

His wicked smile made elation rise in Tommy's chest like a helium-filled balloon even while fear prickled around the edges. "What are you talking about?"

"Apparently, after you repaired Pearl's dishwasher and clothes washer, the handle on her front door broke. She can't lock the door. Opal was insistent that I go over there and fix it, but I really want to help with the goats." His eyes widened in faux seriousness, and Tommy wanted to punch him in the nose and hug him, because he knew what was coming next.

Cash clapped him on the shoulder. "You can thank me later, man. I told Opal you'd be happy to go over there and fix the front door."

Tommy wasn't sure whether to laugh or cry. "I don't know if Pearl's going to like that. She made it pretty clear that I overstepped my bounds by doing dishes and laundry."

"She *needs* this. There is no overstepping repairing a door that won't lock. This is strictly for safety."

"Strictly for safety."

"Right. Opal's getting the information from Pearl, but front door handles and locks are pretty standard, right? I think you can just go to the hardware store and pick something up."

"But shouldn't it be something she likes?"

Cash shrugged. "I think she likes a locking front door."

"I'm not sure this is the best idea. Maybe I should go help Opal, and you should go replace Pearl's front door."

"Oh, no. I'm not doing anything with Pearl's front door. It's all you, man. All you." Whistling, he got in his truck and rolled down the window as he backed out of the parking spot. "Hey, maybe she'll let you in the back door, too. See you later, bro." He made a peace sign and drove off.

Tommy couldn't believe Cash would mention Pearl's back door, and he also couldn't believe his body would react to Cash's suggestion the way it was. His jeans feeling a little snug, he got in his own truck and headed for the hardware store. Just as he parked, his phone chimed with a text from Cash: *Just a heads up. Pearl doesn't know you're coming. She's expecting me.*

Tommy swore and debated sending her a warning message. But he quickly decided against it. If he did, she'd probably tell him not to come, and he didn't want that.

Chapter Seven

Pearl was in approximately minute twelve of yelling at Wyatt
—they'd gotten home after school and he was climbing out
of the car, looking as guilty as a dog with its tail between its
legs—when she noticed Tommy Rowland's truck pulling into her
driveway.

Somehow her completely insane brain managed to think, *This
isn't the only driveway I'd like Tommy Rowland to pull into*, even
while she continued yelling at Wyatt about how she didn't have
time for him to be suspended from school and she couldn't understand why he wouldn't just toe the line for one semester and why
did he have to punch someone?

That's when Wyatt saw Tommy, too. His face flamed bright red,
and Pearl felt the tiniest bit guilty, but only the tiniest bit, because
he deserved to be embarrassed, didn't he? She was embarrassed,
certainly, by the conversation she'd had with Ms. Gutierrez, in
which the kind and soft-spoken teacher had explained that she had
no choice but to suspend Wyatt after he bloodied another kid's nose
and neither of them would say what had caused the fight.

As mad as she was at him, her heart softened at his shame, and
she directed her anger at Tommy as he got out of the car. *If only he*

wasn't such a tall drink of water. Although today, she'd kill for a tall drink of water. Or wine. Or maybe something stronger.

"To what do we owe the pleasure?" She made sure her expression and tone of voice conveyed that his presence was the exact opposite of a pleasure.

He noticed. She saw his Adam's apple bob, and she felt a prickle of guilt when he smiled (and a prickle of desire, too, blast it). He held up a small box. "I've been sent to replace your front door handle."

She opened her mouth and he lifted his other hand to stop her protest. She could swear she saw amusement twinkling in his eyes and because that lessened her resolve, she went to the trunk and started getting out the work she'd brought home.

"Before you say anything, just know that this wasn't my idea. Opal was doing a goat photo shoot with Christmas sweaters and Cash had already promised to help her."

"And you entered into the equation how, exactly?" God, she hated the venom in her voice but she had promised, *sworn* to herself that she wouldn't rely on any man ever again. She had a vague awareness of her sons, standing on either side of her, watching this interaction.

He cleared his throat. "Uh, well, I was at the range with Cash when Opal called. He'd already put off the photo shoot to give me moral support at the range—" he held up his injured hand—"and figured since I'm not working..." He shrugged, looking somewhat bereft.

"Ah." Maybe his arrival really was innocent. "Well, thank you for coming. I didn't want to go to bed with a door that wouldn't lock."

Gah. Why did I reference going to bed?

"Hopefully we can remedy that right now. I'll just get started while you—" he looked around the front yard and then at each boy— "do whatever you're going to do."

The evening suddenly feeling very long and lonely, she sighed. "I'm going to start dinner so it can simmer, and then I'm going to have a talk with my oldest child about punching people in the nose and getting suspended from school. When I'm done with that, I'm going to figure out what to do with said child for the next week while he's out of school and I'm planning a holiday party by myself."

She didn't know why she said it—maybe because she needed an adult to bounce Wyatt's behavior off of. Maybe because, even though she and Leslie hadn't gotten along well for a few years before the divorce, she *was* lonely.

Her words didn't seem to shock Tommy, although his gaze darted to Wyatt and then back to her. "Wow. That sounds ... like a lot of evenings from my childhood. I don't know how my mom made it through, to be honest."

Her shoulders relaxed the tiniest bit. "Well, that's good to know. You turned out fine."

One corner of his mouth lifted. "Thanks."

She groaned and covered her face with her hands. "I'm sorry. That didn't come out right. I'm just—you know what? I'm just going to shut up. Well, first I'm going to thank you for coming to fix the door." She stopped moving and looked him in the eyes. "Thank you. And then I'm going to shut up and leave you alone."

Face burning, she said, "Come on, boys," and walked in through the garage door. After setting her box on the dining room table, she went into the kitchen and started pulling out the ingredients for dinner. Will took off to his bedroom and Wyatt slinked onto a barstool at the counter.

"Want to tell me what happened today?" God, she really had to tone it down, or he'd never talk to her.

His sigh was soul-deep. "Not really. As you know, I punched Leonard Acosta in the face. Gave him a bloody nose."

Pearl froze mid-chop and looked up at Wyatt. "Leonard Acosta? But, *why?* You two have been friends since preschool!"

He didn't answer. Her sweet little boy looked up at her in a way she'd never seen before—a way that made her want to cry. His eyes were serious and shuttered and he wasn't going to tell her a thing.

"Why don't you want to tell me?" Her throat was so tight.

He shook his head, looked down at the countertop, sighed again. Her heart broke.

"It's okay." She swallowed. "You don't have to tell me. Look, I'm sure you had a good reason. And I'm sorry you got in trouble. But you can't go around punching people."

"I don't *go around punching people*, Mom." Again, a side of him she'd never seen. "I punched one person, and trust me, he deserved it."

"Fine. Discussion over. Dinner will be ready in an hour."

Eyes downcast, he slid off the stool and walked away. Her entire body vibrated with a messy mix of emotions ranging from sadness to anger to frustration to worry, and she busied herself with cleaning the kitchen while the meat browned in the pan.

She'd known the boys would eventually stop telling her everything—that was a rite of passage, wasn't it? After wringing out the dishtowel she'd used to wipe down the counters, she started hand-washing the breakfast dishes. So why did it sting like it did? A tear rolled off her nose and into the sink.

"Mom?"

Like a cartoon character caught in a big cry, she used her shoulder to swipe at her cheek. She didn't dare look up. "Yeah?"

"D'you think Mr. Tommy could stay for dinner?"

Her knee-jerk reaction was to blurt out, "No," because the last thing she wanted was company to witness her meltdown. But because she wanted to tread carefully so she wouldn't alienate her kid, who was growing up way too fast, she said, "If he wants to. I mean, I'm sure he has other plans already."

And it was a good thing she chose her response carefully, because a deep voice—a voice belonging to Mr. Tommy himself—answered. "I do want to, and I don't have other plans."

Controlling her startle response was almost impossible, but she did as well as she could and then turned her head, slow motion, to look at him. "You don't have to."

"Consider it repayment for fixing the doorknob?"

Her heart leapt, surprising her—she hadn't realized how stressed she felt about the broken doorknob. She nodded. "Sure. Although, I hope dinner is worth it."

That smile again, nearly erasing the pain of the past few minutes. "It will be."

A while later, the four of them gathered around the table and Pearl prayed the boys would use their manners before reminding herself their dad was unusually strict about it; Tommy wouldn't mind if someone didn't cut a bite small enough or forgot to swallow before speaking.

"Mom, did you know Mr. Tommy got his finger sawed off?"

Pearl nearly choked on her food. "Will, that's very rude to talk about."

His lips pressed together as he tried not to laugh, Tommy set down his fork and knife. "It's okay."

At her single raised eyebrow, he said, "Really. I've been avoiding people because the whole situation is humiliating, so just getting it out in the open is huge."

"One thing kids are great for." Pearl shot Will a dark look. He shrugged.

"Why is it humiliating?" Wyatt wanted to know.

Tommy looked at Pearl, as if asking her permission to answer honestly. She nodded.

"I mean, it's not like I had to get it sawed off for a cool reason, like a shark bit it or an alien stole it for experimentation or a car ran over it while I was saving someone's life. I shut my own finger in a car door. I feel really stupid about it." He looked at each boy and shrugged.

"It's okay." Wyatt reached out and laid one of his hands over Tommy's. "We all do stupid stuff once in a while."

"Wiser words were never spoken," Tommy said. "But hopefully not all of our stupid stuff has permanent consequences."

"Do you think punching Leonard Acosta in the face will have permanent consequences?"

Pearl cringed, but Tommy laughed out loud. "I do. You know what I think the consequence will be? He won't mess with you again."

Wait. Had Wyatt told Tommy what Leonard said, and not her?

Wyatt looked satisfied, and Will said, "But you said it felt good to punch Leonard in the face."

"It did. He deserved it."

"That's enough." Pearl figured she'd better interject before Wyatt said anything violent. After all, Tommy Rowland was an officer of the law. Although she wasn't getting the sense that much ruffled his feathers.

By the time they'd all finished eating, Pearl felt almost back to normal. Then she remembered she still had to find something to do with Wyatt for the next week and felt weary down to her bones.

"Boys, will you please clear the table?"

For the first time in weeks, they hopped to it without complaining or procrastinating. Once they were occupied, Pearl dropped her head into her hands.

"You okay?"

Tommy's concern caused yet another lump to form in Pearl's throat. She raised her head to give him her best impression of a nonchalant expression. "Yes, thank you. I'm fine. Just thinking about what to do with Wyatt while he's suspended. I can't leave him home alone all day. I could bring him to work at June and Sterling's, but I have all these meetings coming up."

"The Peaceful Pines party?"

"The one and only."

A beat of silence passed. Then, "What if I take him?"

"What?" Was he suggesting ...

"What if I keep an eye on him? I mean, I've got nothing going for the next few weeks. Your broken appliances and broken door are the only things that have been keeping me busy—oh, and shooting— and beyond that, I've been bored out of my mind."

"I couldn't possibly ask you—"

"You didn't."

If she wasn't mistaken, the look in his eyes was challenging her. He knew she was in a tough position, knew she didn't have options beyond dragging Wyatt to work with her, and knew she didn't want to accept his help. "You're right. I didn't. You were so kind to offer. But I just can't let you. It's too much." She decided she'd better plow on before she burst into tears again. "Listen. It's been a really nice night, but I'd better get the boys to bed."

Of course, the boys, those little traitors, heard the word bed and jumped to attention.

"But, Mo-om." Will's wail came from the kitchen and Pearl braced herself for what was next. "It's not even seven. We don't go to bed 'til eight-thirty. Can't Mr. Tommy stay a little longer? We told him we were gonna show him our obstacle course in the backyard."

When had they even talked about that?

Tommy cleared his throat. "Um, it's okay. I can come back another time, guys." Then he looked at Pearl like he wasn't sure that was true. "Can't I?"

God, guilt was like a fifty-pound weight on a pendulum and it hit her again. Her sons were craving male attention and letting them show Tommy their obstacle course couldn't hurt. They'd all be in the backyard, anyway, and she wouldn't have to look at his gorgeous face. And why on Earth was she thinking about his gorgeous face?

"It's fine. You guys can show him tonight. I'll finish the clean-up."

The boys pumped their fists and cheered and rushed the back door, calling for Tommy to follow. As he was getting up from his spot at the table, he winked at her, and the gesture actually gave her the warm and fuzzies.

Within seconds, all three of them were laughing and hollering outside, and even as she knew Tommy couldn't entertain her kids all the time, she also realized she hadn't heard them having this much fun in months.

She set down the pan she was scrubbing and went to the sliding door to peek at them. Tommy had put Will on his back and was running away from Wyatt, who held a dart gun in both hands. Tommy rushed around the corner of the play structure, ducking behind the playhouse to shield himself and Will from Wyatt's fire. Just as Wyatt aimed, Tommy stood up and shot Wyatt in the stomach with a foam dart. Wyatt collapsed, playing dead, and Will, still on Tommy's back, pumped his fist and called out in victory.

"Let's go again." Tommy hoisted Wyatt to his feet and pretended to check for bullet wounds.

How many times had Pearl wished Leslie remembered what it was like to be a little boy? If he had, he would have parented Wyatt and Will with so much more patience.

She stepped away from the door and returned to the kitchen so they wouldn't see her watching. Then she turned the water as hot as it would go and scrubbed the pan as hard as she could. The evening was wonderful, but none of them could afford to get attached to Tommy Rowland. Least of all Pearl herself.

Chapter Eight

Pearl calling the next morning was the last thing Tommy expected. She'd made it pretty clear she didn't want his help. And although he understood her need for independence (hadn't he refused to let anyone help him after his surgery?), he also had to force himself to tamp down the disappointment when she said she didn't want him to keep an eye on Wyatt.

The night before, he'd told himself he'd find another way to her heart, and he'd left her house with a pep in his step and a strong, deep desire to kiss her senseless.

Now, it wasn't even seven a.m. and here she was, calling him.

She jumped right in when he answered. "Good morning." Her tone suggested the morning was anything but good, and he said, "Everything okay?"

Her sigh came through the earpiece like a gust of wind. "Everything's fine, but listen. I know I said I didn't want you to help with Wyatt."

"You did say that." Did she reconsider?

"Circumstances have forced me to reconsider."

He shouldn't be doing mental fist pumps right now. Circumstances probably weren't good. But if they were forcing her to let him spend time with Wyatt, and by extension, her, then they were good for him. "What's going on?"

"Well, I was planning to bring Wyatt to work today, but then Will woke up with a fever. I hate to ask you—I asked Opal but she'd already planned a trip down to Phoenix and rented a trailer and rescheduling the whole thing would be a logistical nightmare." The words rolled out quickly, like a tumbleweed on the highway.

"So ..."

"Right. Would it be at all possible for you to stay with the boys today? Like I said, I have a few meetings I have to go to, but I can come home early and finish the day from there. So it won't even be all day. I'll pay you."

"You don't have to pay me. I'd like to hang out with them."

"I'll pay you. I'm desperate."

Oh, how he'd love to hear her use those last two words in bed. He slammed his forehead into his free palm. What was he thinking? He should not imagine Pearl Houston in bed if he was going to babysit her kids. "It's no problem. Really. Remember what I said about being bored out of my mind? I wasn't kidding. This benefits me as much as it does you."

Thirty minutes later, he pulled up at Pearl's house. She rushed out of the garage, giving him a breezy, "Good morning."

Dressed for her meeting, she stopped him in his tracks. He actually froze and took a moment to appreciate the way the gray-blue skirt suit hugged her trim waist and generous hips and managed to show off her cleavage.

"Oh, no. Are you having second thoughts?"

He swallowed. "No. Not at all. Sorry. I've just never seen you in a suit before."

She froze. "Uh oh. Is it bad? I never wear suits."

"No! No, it's good. Really good." He scratched the back of his head. "You look really nice."

A bit of color stained her cheeks. "I do?"

"You do."

They stood there, staring at each other for just long enough that Tommy wondered if he'd overstepped by complimenting her outfit.

Scrambling for a change of subject, he said, "Got any instructions for me?"

The question jumpstarted her into action, and she turned around and headed for the door into the house. "Yes. I wrote down some things, just so I wouldn't forget. I'll show you."

Inside, the boys called out excited greetings from the couch when Tommy came in, and he wondered how sick Will actually felt. He called out a good morning.

Will patted the spot next to him. "Come watch our show with us."

Why was such an invitation so darn heartwarming? "I will, but I've got to look at your mom's instructions, first."

Together, they leaned over the sheet of lined paper on the kitchen counter. "To be honest, I don't know how sick Will actually is. He's acting fine, but since he has a fever, the school nurse will just send him home if I take him in. He does have that glassy-eyed look, but he's bouncing off the walls."

"At that age, excitement over staying home will definitely do that to a person. Even a person with a fever."

Pearl smiled. "So true. Anyway, there's not much—just keep them alive." She gave him a little grimace, pointed at the paper. "You can give Will some medicine in six hours. There's food in the fridge. Don't feel like you have to cook. Wyatt can make lunch."

"Sounds simple enough."

"Please don't let them play video games." She pointed at the spot where she'd drawn a circle with a line through it over *Video games*. "They're not allowed to play when they stay home sick, and Wyatt should not feel like his suspension is a reward."

Tommy nodded, glanced at Wyatt whose set jaw made him look chagrined, and then returned his attention to Pearl. "Anything else?"

She looked at the boys and pressed her lips together. "Promise me you'll give me an honest report on their behavior." She pointed at Wyatt, then at Will. "And you two? No shenanigans."

Will, who was supposed to be sick, jumped to his feet and saluted her. "Yes, ma'am."

And then she was gone and he was left alone with two little kids who stared up at him as if they expected him to know what to do. It was then he realized he should have used his drive time to come up with some kind of a plan for the day. He rubbed his hands together. "So. What do you guys want to do?"

Wyatt shrugged, a much quieter version of himself than the kid who'd come to talk to him the day before while he replaced the doorknob. "We could play a board game, maybe. Or a card game. That's something Mom does with us when we stay home sick."

"What do you like to play?"

Will stretched out on the couch like a cat waking from a nap. "I like to play Monopoly but Wyatt says—"

"It's too boring. It takes so long."

Tommy tended to agree, but didn't say so. "Well, I have an idea for a game, but I'm not sure if you guys are old enough to play." He waved his hand. "Never mind. I doubt you'll want to play it, anyway."

As he'd intended, his feigned dismissal of his own idea made them curious.

"Wait, what is it?" Will sat up.

"Yeah, I don't know about Will, but *I'm* probably old enough."

"I don't know ..." Tommy rubbed his chin. "Are you sure you even want to hear about it?"

Now both boys stood in front of him, pleading with their eyes and their words. "We're sure! Just tell us. We're old enough."

A few minutes later, they sat around the dining room table and Tommy schooled the boys on the basics of poker. He couldn't tell if they totally understood the game, or if they liked it—they did have lots of questions and seemed to put genuine effort into making good hands—but they were engaged and getting along and they weren't playing video games.

After a few hands, they played a game of Monopoly and then Go Fish. It was nearing noon, so Tommy suggested they eat lunch and then watch a movie. They showed him where everything was, and made an assembly line to put the sandwiches together. When they were done, he had them clean up.

"I don't know why we gotta clean up." Will pouted as he swiped at the mustard and mayonnaise Tommy asked him to put away.

"Because we made food. And when we make food, we clean up."

"But we're *guys*."

Those words coming out of Will's tiny body made Tommy want to laugh, but he didn't. "We *are* guys, and the best of us clean up after ourselves."

"We do?"

"We do."

Naturally, they argued over which movie to watch (an argument Tommy remembered well).

"Being a big brother myself," Tommy told Wyatt when Will went to the bathroom, "I hated when my little brother got to pick the movie. But you know what? He's not feeling well, and if we watch the movie he wants to, maybe he'll fall asleep. Then we can put on an older-kid movie."

Wyatt's eyes glinted like they were partners in a conspiracy, and when Will returned to the living room, he announced that Will could pick the movie. Will ran up and gave his brother a big hug. Wyatt threw his arms around Will's shoulders and winked at Tommy over the top of his head.

Still, as the opening music of Will's talking-cars movie played, Wyatt grumbled about having seen it a million times. Will became engrossed immediately, and Tommy took the opportunity to talk to Wyatt.

"Did your teacher give you any schoolwork to do while you're home?"

Wyatt gave him a very adult-like side-eye, and keeping a straight face required all of Tommy's effort. He must have decided he could trust him, because he blew out a breath and said, "Yeah. You gonna make me do it?"

"I mean, it's not on the instructions your mom left, but don't you think she'll be happy if you've done some of the work by the time she gets home?"

"Ugh. She will, but I won't. I don't want to do that stupid schoolwork. It's not my fault I'm suspended."

Tommy shrugged, nonchalant. "Yeah, but wouldn't you have to do the schoolwork even if you weren't suspended?"

"I *guess.*"

"If you don't do some of it today, it's going to stack up, and you're going to spend the weekend doing it. Don't you play soccer?"

The kid's eyes lit up. "Yeah. Hey, you should come to one of my games!"

"Well, if you're not done with your schoolwork, do you think your mom is going to let you play?"

His mouth opened in surprise—apparently, he hadn't thought of that. "Maybe not."

Tommy glanced over at Will, whose blinks were getting longer, and whose body had relaxed into a noodle-like state.

"Why don't you go get it, and we can sit right here and work on it while Will's still awake."

Wyatt trudged from the couch to the hall tree and returned with his backpack. He pulled out a thick manila envelope and turned to Tommy. "Look how nice Ms. Gutierrez was. She made up this whole envelope for me after suspending me for a week."

"So thoughtful," Tommy said, mirroring Wyatt's sarcasm. "Do you have a favorite subject?"

"Um, yeah. P.E. But I guarantee you Ms. G. didn't send home any P.E. Lessons."

"Second favorite?"

"Math, I guess."

"Let's start with that. Although I have to warn you, I'm crap at math."

"Well, I'm not, so you don't have to help me." He opened the envelope and pulled out the whole stack of papers. It seemed like a lot, but Tommy didn't dare say so. By the time Will fell asleep, Wyatt was in the flow, so Tommy let the little-kid movie play.

"This is the paper we started before I punched Leonard." Wyatt held up a worksheet he'd partially completed. "I need to get my history book."

When he returned, setting the book on his lap, Tommy said, "Why'd you punch him?"

Wyatt looked up at Tommy, over at Will, and then down at his book. "He said something about my parents."

Tommy shrugged. "I probably would have punched a kid who said something about my parents, too."

"You would?"

"When I was your age? Yeah. For sure." When Wyatt's shoulders slumped, Tommy rushed to add, "Not that I think punching is okay. But I probably would have, too."

Wyatt grinned up at him, and a weird sensation passed through his body—he *liked* this kid and wanted to protect him from anything that might hurt him, bullies or otherwise.

"Can you tell my mom that?"

Tommy laughed. "Nope."

"Do you promise not to tell her what Leonard said?"

"I'll give you a ninety percent yes. There's certain stuff adults have to tell each other, but if it doesn't fall into that category, I promise not to tell her."

Wyatt nodded, licked his lips, swallowed. "He said my dad left us because my mom is a—well, I'm not even going to say the word. But it starts with an s."

Tommy felt his own hackles rising. Why would any kid say that about another kid's mom? Especially about Pearl, who had to be one of the sweetest moms he knew? He wished he could get face to face with that Leonard Acosta right now. He could see Wyatt's anger returning, too, so he supplied, "Silly person?"

"I wish. But see? You *would* have punched him."

"If I heard him say it today, I'd punch him for sure."

Wyatt's nose wrinkled. "You'd punch a kid?"

"I mean, if *I* was a kid."

"Oh. Because for a minute, I was thinking we should go over to his house after school today and I should ask him to repeat it. So you could hear him say it. And you could punch him right in the nose."

"I'd love to, buddy." He tousled his hair. "But I'm pretty sure I'd lose my job if I did." Holding up his right hand, he added,

"Especially with the finger situation. I can't afford to take any risks."

"Yeah. You're probably right."

"But I'm not going to say you should have done differently." He put a hand on the kid's shoulder. "Family comes first, every time. You defending your mom is always the right thing to do. If the need ever arises again, maybe wait until you're not on school property to punch someone."

Wyatt nodded, serious. The sound of the garage door opening put an end to their conversation. Pearl's voice came through the house as she called, "Hello," and Tommy felt another strange sensation, this one a complete relaxing of his body at Pearl's return to the house. She spotted Will sleeping, first, and put a hand over her heart. "Aw, my little buddy. He's still not feeling well, is he?"

"He insisted on this movie and then slept through all but the first ten minutes."

"Sounds about right." Her gaze landed on Wyatt, who still held his history book on his lap. She gasped. "Are you doing *schoolwork?*"

"Mo-om. Don't act like I never do schoolwork."

"It's just that I didn't hear the sounds of warfare from outside. Yesterday, you said you weren't doing a single assignment while you were suspended. I believe your exact words were, 'I don't *care* if I get behind in school. I'm not even *looking* at what Ms. Gutierrez sent home. If she didn't want me to get behind, she shouldn't have suspended me.'"

Wyatt smiled at what Tommy assumed was exaggerated mimicry, his expression saying, *Caught.* "I might have said that. But I came to my senses when Will insisted on this stupid movie and Mr. Tommy made me sit down and watch it."

Her eyes shone with gratitude when they met Tommy's, and just like the day before, he thought he'd give every single cent he possessed to be the recipient of that look. God, she was beautiful, and he wanted to greet her with a kiss, and he really shouldn't be thinking that way.

"Well, good for Mr. Tommy."

Why did even that turn him on? "It was luck, really."

"Thank you. I wasn't looking forward to coming home and having to force him to get out that envelope."

"There was no force required."

"You must have some magic powers."

Wyatt's head whipped to the side, so he could look at Tommy. "Wait. Did you use magic to get me to do my schoolwork?"

Tommy nodded. "Probably."

"Whatever works." Pearl set down her purse. "You're off the hook now, Mr. Tommy. I can finish today's work from home and keep Wyatt moving on his schoolwork."

Tommy found he didn't want to leave. But he stood up, tousled Wyatt's hair again, and told him, "Keep up the good work. I expect to hear a positive report from your mom."

"Fine."

Smiling, Pearl said, "I'll definitely give you a report. Thank you, again, for watching the kids for me today. I can't tell you how much it means to me. If there's ever anything I can do for you, please let me know. I owe you."

He hoped his thoughts didn't show on his face. "It's no problem. They were really good. They even cleaned up after lunch." He winked at Wyatt, who threw a shady look at his brother (who didn't notice, as he was still sleeping).

Pearl's eyes widened. "You're seriously a miracle worker."

You should see me in bed. What was wrong with him? He needed to get out of here, stat. He offered his hand to Wyatt for a fist bump and said good-bye. As much as it pained him to leave Pearl's company—and the boys'—a satisfied smile came to his face as he thought about her promise to send him a report. Asking for one had been a stroke of genius.

Chapter Nine

What a day. Overall, Pearl considered it a success. Body aching from weariness—she'd hardly slept the night before, as stressed as she was about the day—she pulled on her softest pajamas. Getting ready for bed, she ran through everything that had happened.

Leaving her house that morning, she had to fight the anxiety around leaving Tommy with her kids. Not because she worried about *them*, but because she worried about *him*. When those two boys got to fighting, they sounded like a natural disaster had hit the house. Maybe more than one. A hurricane, an earthquake, and a tidal wave. When she didn't hear from him after an hour, she relaxed a little. When two hours went by, she stopped checking her phone every few minutes.

When she first walked into Pleasant Pines, the giant Christmas tree in the foyer stopped her in her tracks. She still hadn't taken the boys to pick one out. She made a mental note to do that, and by the time she walked into her meeting with the director of Pleasant Pines, Marge, she was able to set that aside, summon her confidence, and announce that she'd be taking over for June. She didn't miss the flicker of disappointment on Marge's face. She felt the wavering of her confidence in a feather-light-but-palpable jolt in every nerve ending.

But then a resident, who introduced herself as Rosa, approached her, asking about June and the baby and Pearl's own plans for the holiday party—and then volunteered to help in any way she could—and Marge's attitude changed. Pearl spent the next hour and a half with Marge and Rosa, planning games, menus, and the hour-by-hour schedule for the holiday party.

Before Pearl left, Marge put a gnarled hand on her forearm. "This is going to be just lovely, honey. I know it."

"Thank you." Tears threatened, but only for a moment.

Marge walked away and Rosa's dark eyes turned beady, and her grip tightened. "The ladies and I, we're expecting perfection. Not a snowflake out of place, you hear? And you'd better make sure there's spiked punch. In a crystal bowl."

Shock made Pearl stammer. "Punch? In a crystal bowl? Spiked? Didn't Marge already say we can't have alcohol?"

Now, Rosa's gaze became even more intense. "Maybe she did, but in case you haven't heard, I'm in charge here, not Marge. And if I say I want spiked punch, I'll have spiked punch. Make sure it's on hand, or you'll never work in this town again."

She hobbled off, and Pearl looked down at the white marks her fingers had left on her arm. Could Rosa really affect Pearl's future as an event planner? Trembling, feeling anything but peaceful, Pearl left Peaceful Pines.

Remembering that moment now, she shuddered as she brushed her teeth. Circumstances improved after that.

She headed back to June's office at the Sweet Springs Ranch. Next, she attended a couple of meetings June had set up before going into labor.

Neither of those—one with the caterer and the other with the florist —involved beady-eyed threats. In fact, Pearl thought they went quite smoothly as she embraced the full decision-making power June gave her.

Finished brushing her teeth, she checked the house one more time to make sure everything was buttoned up. Both boys were asleep in their beds, still covered neatly just as she'd left them. The kitchen was clean, thanks to some weird fluke in which the boys insisted on helping after dinner. And the front door was locked, thanks to Tommy's handyman skills. She turned off all the lights and returned to her bedroom, where she texted June: I haven't gotten my baby fix today. Got any new pictures?

June replied right away with a photo of the baby, Remington, wrapped in a fuzzy red blanket with white snowflakes on it, sleeping soundly.

Pearl: *He's so cute. Makes me miss the baby stage. How are you holding up?*

June: *I'm great. Exhausted but great. So in love.*

Pearl: *That's wonderful. Can I bring you guys dinner one of these evenings?*

June: *Sure. I'd love that. How about tomorrow or the next day?*

Pearl: *The next day is perfect.*

June: *I appreciate it. Thank you.*

The bedroom door swung open and there stood Will, his face flushed. "Mama?"

"Yeah?"

"I think my fever's back. I'm really hot."

Sure enough, his skin was hot to the touch and when she took his temperature the thermometer read 101.4. "You're right, it's back. Let's get you some medicine and some water and get you back to bed."

His immediate compliance was proof of illness, Pearl thought with a smile. As she tucked him back into bed, she realized the return of his fever meant he couldn't go back to school the next day. A groan escaped as she ran through her plans. She could do most of her work from home, but she had afternoon meetings with the DJ and videographer.

Could she leave the boys alone for a couple of hours? No. She banished the thought almost as quickly as she had it. They'd end up accidentally injuring each other ... she pictured them using actual kitchen knives as swords in some alien-dragon battle.

She couldn't possibly ask Opal to watch them, again. Her sister had been beyond helpful but there was such as thing as overstaying your welcome.

Tommy. She had no choice but to ask him. Besides, he'd acted like she was doing him a favor by keeping him occupied.

Before she could chicken out, she typed out a message: *Hey. Will just woke up and his fever is back. Which means I can't send him to school tomorrow. I hate to ask, but do you think you could watch the boys just for a couple of hours tomorrow afternoon? I can work from home in the morning, but I have two meetings I can't reschedule.*

She tapped *Send* and held her breath.

Her eyelids were heavy by the time he responded with, *Of course. What time?*

If she wasn't so set on being independent after her divorce, she'd swoon. He was quite possibly the sweetest man she'd ever met. And her ex-husband's complete opposite.

Pearl: *Thank you a million times. How about 1 pm?*

Tommy: *You're more than welcome. Seriously. Gives me something to look forward to other than my bleak existence.*

Pearl: *It gives me something to look forward to as well. You got Wyatt to do his schoolwork, and whatever you guys talked about made them jump up and help with dinner clean-up this evening.*

Tommy: *What can I say?*

Pearl: *Whatever you already said is perfect.*

Tommy: *I don't want to overstep, but I hope you can find it in your heart to take it easy on him about the punching the kid in the face thing.*

Pearl's breath caught. Had Wyatt shared more with Tommy than he had with her? Suddenly alert again, she sat up straighter in bed.

Pearl: *What did he tell you?*

Tommy: *I'm sworn to secrecy. I'd tell you if it was something that put either of them in danger, but suffice it to say Wyatt was defending his family, and I don't think there's anything more noble than that. Don't worry, I told him punching isn't always the answer.*

Pearl's lips twitched and her posture relaxed. She scooted down under the covers.

Pearl: *You did, did you?*

Tommy: *I also told him that sometimes it is.* He inserted a grimacing emoji. *It's a man's point of view, I know, but I could see where he was coming from. Think about it: that Leonard kid didn't want to tell the teacher why he got punched, did he?*

That was true, he didn't. If he was innocent, he would have shared the story. Maybe Wyatt wasn't a cold-blooded face-puncher, after all. She'd been so worried about both boys since the divorce—even if the parents splitting up was right for the whole family, it was still hard on everyone. Wyatt had been acting out at school ever since. Making "funny" but disruptive comments during class, getting a little too aggressive with other kids while "having fun" on the playground, and even leaving campus one day just to prove he could.

But if whatever happened between Wyatt and Leonard made Tommy think face punching was, in fact, the answer, then maybe she *should* cut Wyatt some slack.

Pearl: *No, he didn't. Maybe instead of having hurt feelings that Wyatt talked to you and not me, I should be glad he opened up to you.*

Tommy: *I'm glad he opened up to me, too. Despite his bravado, he seemed pretty torn up about punching his friend. But his friend deserved it.*

Pearl: *Have you ever punched one of your friends?*

Tommy: *Oh, yeah. And remember - I turned out "fine."*

She was never going to live that down.

Pearl: *I didn't mean it like that.*

Tommy: *I know. Because I turned out amazing.*

Pearl: *I'm not going to argue that fact.*

She glanced at the clock and cringed. It was late, and tomorrow morning was going to come too soon. As reluctant as she was to end the conversation, she knew the Pearl of tomorrow would be grateful for a good night's sleep.

Pearl: *I guess I'd better get to bed. Busy day tomorrow.*

Tommy: *Yeah, me, too. I'm gonna need all the energy I can get to hang out with Wyatt and Will.*

Pearl: *No kidding. Thank you, again. Have a good night.*

Tommy: *You're welcome, again. Goodnight, Pearl.*

She set her phone on the nightstand and snuggled down into her bed. No, she didn't plan on having another romantic relationship—ever—but if she did, it would be with someone exactly like Tommy Rowland.

*   *   *

The next morning, Will woke up right as rain, hurtling into Pearl's bedroom at 6:29 with all the force of a freight train and jumping into her bed. "I'm feeling better, Mom. But I still can't go to school, right? Because I had a fever of one-oh-one last night? So I get to stay home, right?"

Pearl groaned and rubbed her eyes before pulling him down and wrapping him in a hug. "Right. You get to stay home. But I have work to do, so I need you to act sick. Okay? Lay on the couch, talk in a quiet voice, and don't fight with your brother."

Squirming to get out of her embrace, he said, "Okay, Mom. I'm going to get dressed."

"Why don't you go get dressed like this every morning?" she called after him.

He didn't respond. As glad as she was he felt better, she also felt extra guilty about Tommy watching him ... he was firing on all cylinders, which meant babysitting would require a lot of energy.

Even as she debated whether to warn Tommy, she heard a yell from the kitchen. She turned off her alarm, which was set to go off in fifteen minutes, and made her way down the hall. The boys were locked in a battle over the cereal box, faces red, muscles straining as they fought for possession of it.

"Boys!"

"He's going to eat all of it." Will put on his best puppy-dog expression.

"I got it first." Wyatt went for serious, factual.

"There's barely any left."

Will's whining always put Pearl's patience to the test. She walked up to them, her strides fast, and snatched the cereal box from them. "Neither one of you is having cereal this morning. Figure out something else."

With both boys gaping at her, she turned on her heel and carried the box back to her bathroom, where she stuffed it under the sink. After that, she heard nothing but cabinet doors opening and closing and dishes clinking. They were probably in there whisper-arguing, but as long as she couldn't hear it, she didn't care.

The morning passed quickly, with the boys watching TV and playing outside while Pearl began assembling the centerpieces for the Peaceful Pines party. For each one, she had to insert several faux plants, pinecones, and holly berries into a foam tree stump. She'd completed twelve of the twenty she needed when a knock sounded at the door.

"Who's here?" the boys materialized in the living room.

"Mr. Tommy."

"Why is he here?"

"He's watching you while I go to meetings."

A round of shouting and cheering ensued as they raced to answer the door, which they'd thrown open by the time Pearl caught up to them. And there on the doorstep stood Tommy, holding a puzzle, a board game, and a model airplane.

He smiled, gave a little shrug. "Hi. I brought supplies."

The boys fell all over themselves to help him carry in those supplies, and the three of them quickly fell into a discussion about what they'd do first. Feeling extraneous in the best possible way, Pearl packed up, bid them good-bye, and left. She told herself that her rush to get out of the house had everything to do with getting to her meeting a few minutes early, and nothing to do with getting away from Tommy and how he made her feel ... like she just might be able to fall for someone, after all.

Chapter Ten

Tommy Rowland was sitting on Pearl Houston's back patio, and they were sharing a bottle of wine. He was at once thanking his lucky stars and doing his best to ensure this wasn't a one-and-done experience.

Because as much as his face stung from the cold, it was nice. Really, really nice.

The sun had gone down a while ago, but a faint, silvery light silhouetted the horizon. The night was silent; no insects or birds braved the winter temperatures that made Tommy's fingertips numb. And Pearl. In the glow of the string lights hanging from the eaves, she leaned against the back of her Adirondack chair, her glass in one hand, her hair slightly messy, her features the most relaxed he'd seen since fixing the dishwasher and washing machine. And she was beautiful.

Watching her as a mom was one thing—she was fun and funny and warm and sometimes stern. But watching her at the end of the day, while her kids were tucked into bed, was something else entirely. With the golden light on her face, she looked like she'd come straight from the sky itself. She'd draped a thick blanket over her lap and offered to share it with him, but he declined. He preferred the biting cold to being that close to Pearl and unable to touch her. She offered to get him another from inside, but he was afraid she'd wake the boys and their alone time would come to an end.

"Thank you again for staying with the boys today. I feel like I owe you way more than a glass of wine." Again, his traitorous mind concocted several ways in which she could repay him, and he was even more glad he'd chosen not to share her blanket.

"You're welcome. They were easy."

She arched an eyebrow at him.

"Really! They were good."

"Why are they always good for other people?"

"They're hiding their secret identities as supervillains."

She laughed out loud at that, and the sound was like the sweetest praise. "I've never heard such a good answer."

He smiled.

"I get to go see June and Sterling's baby tomorrow. I told her I'd bring them dinner."

"I think I'm supposed to say, 'That's great,' but can I tell you a secret?"

"Ooh, I love a good secret." She grinned at him, wicked, and he couldn't help but imagine her looking at him like that between the sheets.

"I'm terrified of babies."

Again, laughter that made his heart beat faster. "You are? They're so tiny. What's there to be afraid of?"

"That's exactly it! They're so tiny! And fragile. And everyone says how cute they are, but they look like wrinkly little worms!" She didn't answer right away and he rushed to say, "Oh, no. Now I've gone too far."

"No, you haven't. Your honesty is refreshing. I have to admit, I love babies. I kind of miss that stage, when they can't talk back or punch their friends in the face."

"But they can cry."

Pearl shrugged. "True. Still love 'em. So I guess we can agree to disagree."

"Fair enough. How were your meetings today?" It was the first time they'd had a chance to discuss adult topics; once she got home, they talked about Wyatt's schoolwork, Will's continued lack of a fever and improved appetite, and whether Tommy would stay for dinner (at the kids' request). Throughout the evening, the boys fought for his attention, showing off magic tricks and crazy jumps off the couch and cool toys. Not that he minded. He got a kick out of the boys and their shenanigans.

"They were good. Better than yesterday's."

"Why? What happened yesterday?"

"Let's just say one of the Peaceful Pines residents threatened everything but my life if I don't provide spiked punch at the holiday party."

Tommy's eyebrows shot up. "Not the kind of interaction I'd expect at Peaceful Pines."

"Same."

"Did you tell June?"

"No!" She sounded scandalized. "I can't tell her. I don't want her to stress over the party. I've got everything handled. Except maybe the eight million snowflakes I have to assemble before then."

"Did the spiked-punch lady say anything about the snowflakes?"

"Not yet. But I'm sure she will."

"Want me to have a word with her?" He did his best to look menacing.

"Ha. Yes, please. Her name's Rosa, and you'll recognize her by her beady eyes and talon-like claws. She actually left marks on my arm, she was squeezing it so hard."

"Wow."

"I know."

They settled into a comfortable silence, and to his surprise, Tommy let himself envision many future nights like this one. Which unsettled him. He rarely envisioned future nights with women.

Maybe I should go.

"I guess the good news is that Will can go back to school tomorrow. So you're off the hook."

Even though he'd just been thinking he should leave, the fact that she wouldn't need his help the next day sent a wave of disappointment over him. "That is good news. I'm glad he's feeling better."

"Can *I* tell *you* a secret?"

"Of course. It's only fair that you tell me one, since I told you one."

"I never want the kids to feel sick. But sometimes, when they do get fevers or whatever, and they just want to lay around and cuddle? I enjoy that. I like that they need me."

"I get that."

"Do you think it makes me a bad person?"

He wanted to kiss away the line that formed between her brows. "Nah. Those two are full of energy, for sure. I remember going a million miles an hour as a kid. Sometimes I would finally get in bed and realize I hadn't sat down all day. I also remember my mom complaining that my siblings and I always operated at full speed. 'If they're not bouncing off the walls and beating the snot out of each other, they're sleeping.'"

"Doesn't surprise me."

"What does that mean?"

She grimaced a little, as if she hadn't meant to say what she did. "Do I have to say?"

"Now you do," He winked at her to keep the tone light.

"We've known each other for a while now."

"We have." He'd watched her go from absolutely broken when she and her ex decided to divorce to quietly hurting and then to more calm and confident in the past few months. But what had she observed about him? He hadn't even considered that.

"You love being busy, right?"

"Right."

"And this whole finger thing—" she inclined her head—"and not being able to move at your usual pace ... it's throwing you for a loop, right? You feel like you've lost your purpose, even if it's temporary, and you hate it."

"Yikes. You really nailed it." He wasn't sure whether he liked that she'd nailed it. Her astute observations made him want to squirm. But also, she had observations. She'd paid attention to him over the past year as they'd come into each other's orbits through Cash and Opal.

She simply waited, compelling him to go on.

Simultaneously shy about opening up and craving this connection as it unfolded between them, he chose his words carefully. "You're right. I feel like I've lost my purpose. And although it's supposed to be only temporary, like you said, part of me worries it's not."

She quirked an eyebrow. "Why wouldn't it be?"

"What if I can't learn to shoot another way? They'll medically retire me or put me behind a desk. I'm not sure what's worse." Speaking that fear out loud made it hard to breathe.

Pearl reached across the space between them and placed a hand on his. When their eyes met, the gentle kindness in hers unlocked that tight feeling in his chest and his lungs filled with air again. He couldn't look away; the contact transfixed him.

"I can see how that would be terrifying."

"You can?"

She shrugged, but didn't take her hand off his. "Of course. It's obvious how much you love being a cop. The way Cash talked about training with you, I get the impression you're good at it. And something like this, something that threatens the career you've obviously built your life around? Yeah. Pretty terrifying."

He couldn't believe how good it felt to hear those words. Then she said, "But," and his heart sank. "Don't underestimate yourself, Tommy Rowland. I'm certain you're capable of learning to shoot another way if it means that much to you."

His name on her lips did something crazy to him. It made him want to throw himself at her feet and offer to do whatever she asked, forever. "Thank you." The words weren't nearly enough to express his gratitude, to tell her how much her encouragement meant.

She squeezed his hand. "You're welcome." Still, she didn't let go.

He was sitting on Pearl Houston's back patio, in one of her Adirondack chairs, and she was holding his hand. She'd made the first move, even. The little-boy version of Tommy, who showed up in his consciousness every now and then, did a fist pump and whispered, "Yessss."

The adult version held as still as he could, with the exception of using his free hand to lift his wine glass to his mouth. Casual. Nonchalant. As if Pearl's hand on his was no big deal, even though his heart was beating out a rhythm of content he hadn't experienced in ages. Maybe ever.

"Mom?"

Tommy realized he hadn't even registered the sound of the glass door sliding open, but Wyatt's voice startled him and Pearl, and she snatched her hand off his. Icy air replaced the warmth of her touch.

"Yeah?" Pearl turned around to look at Wyatt, and Tommy did, too, hoping the kid hadn't seen the hand-holding. It'd probably be awkward for a kid to see his mom holding hands with someone.

"Do I have to go to work with you tomorrow?"

"Yes. Now go back to bed."

Wyatt rubbed his eyes and a surge of affection made Tommy's heart twist. As much as he tried to act like the cool big brother, he was still just a little kid.

"But I don't want to. It's going to be so boring."

"Consider it part of your punishment for punching Leonard Acosta." She turned around, conveying the conversation was over.

Wyatt had other ideas: he came up and leaned against Pearl, his cheek resting on the top of her head. "He deserved it, Mom. I'm telling you. Didn't he, Tommy?"

Tommy held up his hands in shock and innocence. "I'm staying out of this."

Wyatt shook his head, the disappointment palpable, and Tommy almost couldn't believe how much that stung. He'd intended to stay out of it—he'd never interfere with a mother disciplining her child—but Pearl raised an eyebrow at him.

"What does Mr. Tommy know that I don't, Wyatt?"

Ooh, she was good. And he felt bad for Wyatt. He was definitely not going to want to tell Pearl what Leonard Acosta—the little jerk—had said about her.

"I know you think you wanna know, but you don't, Mama. I'm twelve now. Can you just trust me that he deserved it?"

Tommy could see Pearl softening, her shoulders relaxing, her head tilting toward Wyatt.

Ooh, he was good, too. Then he slipped up. "He's lucky all I did was punch him in the face. If I had more time, I would have punched him the kidneys, too, and I would have kicked him in the—"

"That's enough, Wyatt. Yes, you have to go to work with me."

Wyatt's shoulders slumped, but only for a moment. He stood up straight. "Can't I stay with Mr. Tommy again?"

"It's late. Get to bed." Pearl wrapped an arm around Wyatt's waist and squeezed. "Goodnight. Again."

Wyatt hugged her back around the shoulders. "Mr. Tommy, you got plans tomorrow?"

Tommy looked at Pearl and then at Wyatt. "I mean, no. I don't. But your mom already said you have to go to work with her."

Another dramatic shoulder slump. Then it was as if Pearl suddenly remembered what Tommy said about giving Wyatt a break.

"You know what? I guess we could ask Mr. Tommy if he wants to hang out with you. Maybe you could come with me to work for a while and hang out with him for part of the day. I just don't want you to feel like being suspended is fun."

Tommy couldn't help the grin that came to his face, lightning fast. He winked at Tommy. "I'm not busy tomorrow. And I promise that if you hang out with me, we will not have any fun. Not even a little."

Wyatt grinned, and Pearl did, too.

"Aren't you bringing dinner to June and Sterling tomorrow?"

Pearl nodded. "I'm making a casserole, but I need to go to the store to grab fresh bread and salad."

He may as well be throwing himself off a cliff. "What if I keep Wyatt tomorrow and pick up Will from school? That will give you a little extra time to do your work and go to the store. And if you want,

I can stay with them while you deliver the food to Sweet Springs. That way they don't give the baby their gross little boy germs."

Wyatt wrinkled his nose. "Hey! I bet I have less germs than that baby! Babies are *gross*!"

"I happen to agree with you, but be careful, your mom thinks they're cute. And let's be realistic: you and Will, who go to school and soccer every week, have way more germs than a newborn baby."

Wyatt huffed. "Fine. You're probably right. So, Mom? Can we do what Mr. Tommy said?"

There was that connection again, hitting him in the gut and permeating every single cell in his body. "Sure. That sounds reasonable. But you'd better thank Mr. Tommy for saving you from an entire day of boredom."

Without warning, Wyatt threw himself at Tommy, wrapping his arms around Tommy's head and squeezing it. Tommy set down his wine and returned the embrace with both arms. A guy didn't give a one-armed hug to a kid expressing gratitude.

"We are really going to owe you, Mr. Tommy," Pearl said.

He couldn't wait to collect.

Chapter Eleven

"**A**nd then Wyatt went to bed and Tommy said he should probably get going and we stood there and looked at each other for so long, and I thought we were going to kiss." Pearl could hear the teenaged-girl angst in her own voice and wanted to laugh, even though she'd rehashed that moment about a gazillion times since the night before.

June sat on her couch inside the Sweet Springs Ranch's big house, baby Remington in her arms—and a glint in her eyes. "So you're telling me that you have the hots for Tommy, he has the hots for you, and it's only a matter of time until you both do something about it."

Pearl's cheeks flushed. "That might be what I'm telling you."

June emitted a little squeal, and the baby stirred, making both women laugh.

"I mean, what are you going to do about it?"

"*Do?*" Pearl flung her hands up. "Nothing! I can't date! I have two little boys to think of."

June raised an eyebrow. "Two little boys who, from what I hear, very much enjoy spending time with Mr. Tommy, who also happens to seem to enjoy spending time with them."

Pearl sighed.

June stood up. "Here. Hold this baby while I heat up the dinner."

"I want to hold the baby, but let me get the dinner in the oven for you, and then I'll hold him."

"Please." June held out the baby like an offering. "I could use a break."

Hearing an edge to her friend's voice, Pearl took the baby and nestled him against her chest. She melted at the little snuffling sound he made. "Tired of having a ninety-eight-degree heating pad attached to you at all times?"

June's back faced Pearl as she preheated the oven, and her shoulders moved up and down with a big sigh. "Yes. Which I haven't been able to say to anyone else. But you understand, right?" She spun around, her eyes wide waiting for Pearl's response.

Even as she smiled, tears sprang to Pearl's eyes. "I do. I completely understand. Babies are hard work and you're sleep deprived and sometimes they just cry and cry unless you're holding them. It's exhausting even at the best of times. And I still miss it."

June put the baking dish in the oven, and when she turned around, she put her forearms on the counter and her head on her forearms, and started to cry. Big, loud sobs that made Pearl's heart ache, because she could remember the vast feelings that accompanied having a newborn. The deep love, the fear, the bone-deep exhaustion, the inadequacy.

Holding the baby in one arm—how natural it still felt even after all this time—she moved around the counter and wrapped her other arm around June's shoulders. "It gets easier. I promise. They cry less and they can ask for what they want and they eventually use the toilet. And then they go around punching other kids in the face at school."

As she'd intended, that last bit made June laugh, and June stood up and clung to Pearl, both of them half-crying and half-laughing. When the emotions finally subsided, Pearl gave June's shoulders one more squeeze and reached for the box of tissues.

"I'm sorry," June said, taking one and dabbing her eyes. "I'm just such a mess."

Pearl laughed through her own tears. "It's fine. Look at me. I remember the newborn days so well. It's bittersweet. I promise, you can do this. You're a great mom already, and you're only going to get better with practice."

The sobbing had stopped, but apparently the tears continued to flow, because June grabbed another tissue and dabbed her eyes again. "I know. It's just so ... *hard.* And I'm so tired. And I can't take a shower without him squalling like an actual tornado. I know Sterling will take him whenever I ask, but I'd love to be clean when he gets home from his errands. But no matter what I do, I can hear Remington screaming when I'm in the shower."

Pearl remembered the rushed showers like they were yesterday. Maybe Sterling would take Remington, but Pearl's ex, Leslie, rarely volunteered for baby duty when Pearl wanted to shower or, God forbid, take a moment to herself. With Opal on the other side of the country and their parents retired in Florida, Pearl didn't feel like she had anyone to help.

She decided then and there that June wouldn't feel that way. "You know what? Go shower. I've got this guy until you get done. Don't rush. Lather up that body pouf, enjoy the hot water, and *really* shampoo your hair. Take your time putting on your lotion and drying your hair if you want to."

Tears filled June's eyes again. "No, I couldn't. Your boys are home, and I know you don't like to leave them unattended for too long."

"They're not unattended! Tommy's with them." She realized the mistake as soon as the words left her mouth.

June's eyes, as watery as they were, narrowed. "Wait. Tommy's with Wyatt and Will? I'd rather sit down and get all the tea than take a boring *shower.* How did *this* come about?" She sank onto a barstool and propped her chin on her hands.

Pearl flapped a hand at her, gesturing toward the hallway. "I'll tell you after you shower. Get going, before this baby gets hungry, because if that happens, there's only so much I can do to keep him quiet."

That did the trick, and June threw over her shoulder, "Fine! But

I'm no longer taking a long, luxurious shower! I can't wait to hear the scoop. This has been brewing for a while now!"

Once she was gone, Pearl carried the baby to the couch and sat down to admire his tiny fingers and fingernails, and the sweep of his dark, thick lashes (which were definitely a Wilder family trait). Remington had a ton of hair for a baby, and Pearl ran her fingertips through it, creating little spikes, making him turn his head this way and that.

She texted Tommy: *I'm on baby duty just long enough for June to shower, and then I'll head home. I hope that's okay. Remington cries whenever she puts him down. Tugged at my heartstrings. If you have somewhere to be, it's totally fine to leave the boys for a bit.*

Tommy: *Sounds good. I'm holding down the fort here. Take your time. We're in the middle of fighting off a space invasion. Not to worry, I've got the best dragon.*

Pearl's smile was involuntary. *Wonderful. Good luck to you. Let me know if you need backup. And will you remind Wyatt he was going to put dinner in the oven?*

Tommy: *My commander says this is man's work. You can heat up dinner when you get home.*

Pearl: *I take it your commander is a sixth grader, about five-foot, two inches tall?*

Tommy: *One and the same. He's less intimidating than he thinks he is, so he may be begging for your forgiveness when you get home, if I've taken my dragon and turned against him and his army.*

She shouldn't compare—no one could compare with Leslie Marshall—but she couldn't remember a time Leslie even pretended to be interested in the boys' make-believe games.

Pearl: *Please inform your commander that if dinner isn't in the oven by the time I get home, he's making dinners for the next week.*

Tommy: *Roger that. I've got to go. I've got a secondary attack coming from the south.*

Pearl: *Good luck.*

Tommy: *Don't need it. I've got skillz.*

"Wow. Not only is Tommy home with your kids, but he's also making you smile like *that*."

June, clean and wearing fresh clothes, returned to the living room, running a comb through her hair.

Pearl dropped her phone—which she recognized as a sign of guilt. "Smile like what?"

Laughing, June said, "Like you're smitten. So are you?" She sank down onto the couch. "Also, why does he sleep so well whenever anyone else is around? You all are going to think I'm crazy, the way I talk about him not sleeping."

"Wyatt was the same way. I was such a nervous first-time mom. I'm sure he picked up on it." Although years had passed, Pearl could literally feel the anxiety, the gritty eyes, and, of course, the overwhelming love she'd felt for her little boy.

"You were?"

"I was."

"Look at you now."

Pearl laughed. "Yeah. Twelve years and two babies later, and I can give this guy back if he starts crying."

June sighed. "Yeah."

"You're doing great, June." Pearl put a hand on June's knee. "He's fed and he's clean, and he has everything he needs."

"Thank you. I appreciate it. Anyway. Enough about me. I should ask about the Peaceful Pines holiday party, but truth be told, I'm too tired for work mode and I'm way more interested in how Tommy ended up at your house, watching the boys."

Pearl had already decided not to talk to June about the Peaceful Pines party any more than strictly necessary—she wanted her to be able to focus on the baby. She gave her the short version of how Tommy ended up watching the boys when Will got sick, and added in how they'd sat outside with glasses of wine the night before and how he'd texted just then about the alien invasion and dragons.

With each new detail, June's smile widened. "He is totally smitten with you, Pearl."

Pearl felt her face heat. She was blushing—actually *blushing*, which she hadn't done in as long as she could remember. "He might be smitten with my boys, but he's not smitten with me."

"Yes, he is."

"No, he's not."

The front door opened, and Sterling came in.

"Yes, he is." June pointed at Pearl.

"No, he's not."

"Who is what?" Sterling walked over to the couch to plant a kiss on June's lips.

"Tommy Rowland is smitten with Pearl."

"He's not." Pearl gave Sterling a serious look.

"He is." June gave Pearl a serious look.

June relayed the story of how Tommy had ended up watching Wyatt and Will, and when she finished, Sterling winked at Pearl. "He is." Pearl shook her head and Sterling said, "Smells good in here."

"Pearl brought dinner. She even held Remington while I showered, so I could be fresh and clean for you."

"No wonder Tommy's smitten with her." Sterling winked at Pearl, who shook her head.

"He's not now, but he definitely won't appreciate me taking too long to relieve him from the alien-dragon war in which he is currently embroiled."

She held the bundled-up baby out to Sterling, who took him, kissed him on the forehead, and expertly tucked him into the crook of his arm. Before standing up, Pearl reached over to give June a hug. "Hang in there, Mama. It gets easier."

"Thank you. And thank you for dinner. It smells heavenly."

"It's no problem. We're having the same thing—I just made double."

"Are you trying to make Tommy even more smitten with you?" Sterling wanted to know. "Because if this is cooking at your house, too, it's going to work."

With a final, good-natured eye roll, Pearl returned to her car. Were June and Sterling right? Was Tommy really smitten with her? She started the car and backed down the long gravel driveway. She'd been away from the dating scene for going on a decade and a half now, and hadn't even thought about the signs that someone might be smitten with her in all that time.

Turning onto the main road, she considered.

The other night at Opal and Cash's, he'd seemed to sense when she was feeling down, and made a joke to cheer her up. But wouldn't any decent person do that for the sister-in-law of one of his closest friends?

And he had repaired her dishwasher and washing machine, but again, wouldn't any decent person do that for someone in his circle? He'd watched the kids a few times now, but he'd done that because he liked *them*. It had nothing to do with her, did it?

Almost home, she decided she'd pay extra attention to how he acted. If he did, in fact, have feelings for her, she'd have to nip them in the bud immediately. She wasn't on the market. Was she?

The first thing she noticed when she walked through the door was the smell of dinner cooking. Which meant someone (hopefully Wyatt) had put it in the oven. A certain calm settled over her. Maybe (thanks in part to Tommy's nudging) she could train the boys to participate in home life, even if their dad hadn't modeled it.

"I'm home!" As she set down her purse, she noticed a strange silence, which could mean only one thing: the boys were hiding somewhere, waiting to ambush her with their dart guns or the fake snowballs she'd bought them.

When she walked into the living room, though, not a single object came flying through the air at her. Instead, she heard their calls of, "Surprise!" at the same time she saw the giant Christmas tree standing in the corner. It was probably the biggest one she'd ever seen, and she saw dollar signs right away. Leslie would never let them get a tree that big—or that expensive.

The boys emerged from behind it and came running at her, throwing their arms around her waist. Tommy came out of hiding, too, and stood next to the tree, his expression hopeful and uncertain.

"Surprise," he said, his eyes on hers, gauging her reaction.

And that's when she knew: June and Sterling were right. Tommy *was* smitten with her.

Chapter Twelve

The look on Pearl's face when she saw the Christmas tree was everything. Then Tommy saw the boys rush her. When she embraced them both and grinned at him over their heads—*that* was everything. Her gratitude flew across the room and hit him square in the chest, palpable. If they'd been alone, she would have embraced him. Hell, she probably would have kissed him. Damn, he wished they were alone.

But working with Wyatt and Will to plan the whole surprise for Pearl had been almost as great as seeing her reaction.

He'd spent quite a bit of time and brain power thinking about what he was going to do with the two of them while Pearl went to her meetings and brought dinner to June and Sterling. The tree idea hit him when he and Wyatt left the house to pick up Will. One of their neighbors was stringing lights on a great big blue fir tree in the front yard and Wyatt said, "I wonder when we're going to get our tree. We always get it right after Thanksgiving, but Mom's been so busy with her new job, we haven't had time."

The kid sounded so wistful. He put on a brave face, but Tommy could tell he was worried they weren't getting a tree at all.

"You know what? Why don't we go get Will, and then go pick out a tree? We can surprise your mom."

Wyatt's attention snapped over to Tommy, his eyes alight with hope. "That's a great idea!" His shoulders slumped, then. "But d'you think Mom will be sad she doesn't get to pick it out?"

Tommy hadn't thought of that. He considered. "I think she might be a little sad, just for a minute. But then I think she'll be excited you guys have a tree and she can cross that off her list. She's been so busy, like you said."

Wyatt nodded. "I think you're right. But we need to feed Will, first. He's always hangry after school, and if we don't feed him, he'll ruin the tree shopping."

"Done."

They picked up Will and swung through the Donut Shop drive-through for sandwiches. While they waited, Tommy told the boys about the time he and Cash had to talk Umbrella Jack out of walking through the drive-though a year before.

"That's awesome! Can we walk through?" Will wanted to know.

Tommy shook his head. "I'm afraid my storytelling might have backfired. It's actually against the rules to walk through."

Of course, they wanted to know why, and Tommy didn't really know, but the cashier handed out their sandwiches and they were on their way to the Christmas tree lot.

"Before we get out of the car, I need to tell you guys something." Both boys looked at him, eyes serious. "We're not going to argue over the tree, okay? Doing something nice for somebody, like we're doing right now for your mom, is for mature kids only."

"What's mature?" Will asked, his mouth full.

"Swallow before you talk." Wyatt's eyes flicked to Tommy and back to his brother, and Tommy remembered the stories Cash had told him about their dad getting pissed off if they neglected their manners.

"Mature is when you act more grown-up. When you picked out Christmas trees before, did your mom or dad ever argue over it?" The words were out of his mouth before he realized, and he prayed Pearl's ex had at least been mature enough not to argue over a Christmas tree (he had tipped over an entire dining room table once, if Tommy remembered correctly).

"They didn't," Will said. "They always let us choose."

Tommy breathed a sigh of relief. "That's because they're mature."

"*We* might have argued." Will's voice was quiet, guilty.

"Sometimes kids argue. But not today, all right? You've grown out of that now." Tommy reached into the backseat and patted his knee.

Wyatt threw Tommy a doubtful look. "Let's hope so."

"Hey. None of that. Let's go."

Finding the right tree didn't take long. The boys ran up or down every aisle in the lot, examining the ones with the close-together branches and the far-apart branches, and the ones with the strong scent and the mild scent, and within a few minutes had decided on what had to be the tallest tree there. *Of course.* Tommy probably would have wanted that one when he was a kid, too.

Although he knew the price was going to be outrageous, he went ahead and asked the attendant to load it up. Will and Wyatt had navigated the selection process so seamlessly, he couldn't ask them to choose a different one.

He quickly determined the tree was worth the cost. The two boys were giddy as the attendant put on the netting and helped Tommy carry the tree out to the truck. When they returned to the house, Wyatt volunteered to get the tree stand from the garage and Will filled a pitcher with water.

Tommy hadn't anticipated the difficulty of getting the giant tree out of the truck and into the house with two kids as helpers, but Wyatt proved strong enough to carry the top end and Will seemed to enjoy "steering" them into position. Then there was the whole matter of making the tree stand up straight. From one end of the living room, Will gave direction while Wyatt held the tree and Tommy adjusted the screws in the base. He estimated that process took about three years (maybe more like ten minutes, but it felt like years), as rushed as he was to get it done before Pearl came home.

Once they were done, the boys danced around in celebration, giving each other and Tommy high fives, and then giving each other even more high fives, until they collapsed in fits of giggles. Their joy was contagious, and Tommy found himself caught up, giggling along with them, beyond excited to see Pearl's reaction to their surprise.

Then Pearl texted that she was going to hold Remington while June showered, and it felt like another six years (or thirty minutes) before she finally walked through the door.

And oh, was all the work worth it.

"You guys got a Christmas tree?" she finally said, the pitch of her voice at an all-time high, and more high-fiving and giggling commenced.

"No, Mom." Will squealed. "We got a Christmas *cactus*."

"Are you *crying*?" Wyatt grabbed Pearl's wrist and examined her face.

Pearl laughed. "I might be a bit misty-eyed. This is just such a nice surprise."

"It was Mr. Tommy's idea," Wyatt said, and Tommy used all of his will power to stop himself from saying, "Aw, shucks" when she looked at him with those shining eyes.

And then she rushed across the room and hugged him, and he knew he'd never be the same. He was all wrapped up in her gratitude and her excitement and her woodsy, floral scent and he put his arms around her waist and inhaled and never wanted to let go.

"Thank you." Her whisper sent shivers rushing through his body, making him aroused in a whole new way. In fact, he should release her immediately, but he found he couldn't. "It's too much. Way too much. But it's wonderful. Thank you."

He remembered she'd thanked him and it had been several seconds. "You're welcome."

Finally, she ended the embrace and squeezed his shoulders one more time before dropping her hands to her sides. "Stay for dinner. The least I can do to thank you is to feed you."

"I won't turn down a meal that smells as good as this casserole does."

She gave him one more smile before turning to the boys. "Should we have Mr. Tommy help us decorate the tree?"

He should protest. Surely decorating the tree was a family activity, and he wasn't family even if he had commandeered the tree surprise. But when the boys started jumping around, cheering, their fists in the air, he found himself saying, "I'd love to."

And just like that, he was wrapped up in the evening's action, helping dish up the dinner, clear the table, choose the holiday music, pull out the decorations, and decorate the tree.

When they were done and had toted the empty ornament boxes back out to the garage, Pearl told the boys to get ready for bed, promising them a special surprise if they were both in bed with teeth brushed by the time she and Tommy finished a glass of wine.

"Why do you guys keep having a glass of wine?"

"I can tell from your whiny voice that you're getting tired." Pearl shooed him toward the hallway.

"But you never did that with Dad."

Pearl quickly schooled the shock off her face and smiled. "Dad never had time, Will. Now get to bed."

He zipped off, responding to the razor's edge in her voice. Wyatt offered Tommy a fist bump and another thank you before he, too, disappeared down the hallway.

"You're obviously a saint," Pearl said as she pulled the cork from the bottle they'd opened the night before. She poured, then handed him a glass. "But you almost certainly could use a glass of wine after spending the entire afternoon with those two."

They walked across the living room, where the tree stood in the corner, lit and shining with ornaments. Pearl sat on the loveseat and patted the cushion next to her. Once he sat down, she put her hand on his, just as she had before. She waited for him to look at her before she said, "Thank you. Really. You have no idea how much it means that you took Wyatt and Will to get a tree."

His heart aflutter, he smiled. "You're welcome. I couldn't shake how sad you looked the other night at Cash and Opal's when you mentioned you hadn't gotten one yet." He didn't tell her he hadn't been able to erase that image from his mind until he fixed it.

"I *was* sad. And what's worse is that a tree didn't cross my mind again after that—I've been so busy and so stressed. But then today, when I walked in and saw it there—" her voice cracked—"I realized I'd forgotten to think about it, and was so relieved you'd picked up the slack. If you left me to my own devices, I might have forgotten all together, and then the boys wouldn't have had a tree."

"And you wouldn't have, either."

She smiled. "You're right. Christmas is supposed to be all about the kids, but I would have been disappointed, too. I can't tell you how much I love sitting in the living room at night, the tree all lit up, a fire in the fireplace, a glass of wine or spiked eggnog in hand."

And cue the movie reel of Tommy laying Pearl down on the rug in front of that fire, kissing her senseless, and removing every item of her clothing, piece by piece. "This is really nice." Did his voice sound as strangled as it felt?

It must not, because she intertwined her fingers with his. "It is."

They both jumped, releasing each other's hands, when one of the boys called, "Mo-om." Tommy was so wrapped up in his reaction to Pearl that he couldn't discern which boy it was. Pearl leapt to her feet. At the mouth of the hallway, she turned around and flashed him a grin. "Hold that thought. I'll be right back."

Time seemed to stretch while she was gone, leaving him with the space to think about whether getting wrapped up in this whole situation was a good idea. Will's words, delivered with an accusatory tone, "You never did this with Dad," remained fresh in Tommy's memory.

What would the boys think of a romance between their mom and Tommy? What if they hated it? What if their dad made his life a living hell out of jealousy? The thoughts were like a freight train, gathering momentum in his brain.

But then Pearl reemerged from the hallway, and the thoughts and the train they were on dissolved into thin air. Because she was just so damn beautiful in the light from the Christmas tree, her hair up in a messy, end-of-the-day 'do, and her eyes on his while she smiled like she'd never been happier to see someone.

"Hi."

He stood, his body moving of its own accord. The two of them moved toward each other, the air between them suddenly alive, urging them closer. Pearl didn't slow down when she reached him—

she wrapped her arms around his waist and he wrapped his around her shoulders.

"Thank you for today." Her face was just centimeters from his. "Actually, thank you for this week. I couldn't have survived without you."

"I'm pretty sure that's a slight exaggeration. You're one of the most capable women I know, Pearl Houston."

"But this week, I didn't have to be. And that means more than you know."

Her hands slid up his back and the distance between them closed. Her lips were on his and he was positive he'd never tasted anything so sweet. She broke the contact, just briefly, and then pressed her lips against his again, this time letting hers part. A groan escaped him and he brushed his tongue against hers. In response, she whimpered and tightened her hold on him, taking the kiss deeper.

The kiss itself was like being just outside the gates of paradise. It was so, so good … and yet he could sense there was even more. He could go on like this forever and also he could never get enough. His own hands moved, too, cupping her face, running through her hair. His arousal pressed against his jeans and his jeans pressed against her waist and he didn't know whether to be embarrassed or even more aroused, but then she reached between them and stroked him and he leaned into her touch and moved his palms to her breasts and she moaned in pleasure.

"Maybe we should get out of the living room." Her words, close enough to his own mouth he could feel them, brought him only halfway out of his drugged state.

He nodded, kneaded her breasts, kissed her neck. "I'm sure you're right. Where should we go?" Her fingertips were in his waistband, and he throbbed for her.

"Outside?"

"Let's go." Incredibly turned on by the fact that he felt like they were a couple of teenagers sneaking a make-out session, he grabbed her hand and headed for the door. The chill hit his skin immediately, and when Pearl shivered, he grabbed a blanket off the Adirondack chair, wrapped it around her shoulders, and held onto its corners to pull her against him.

They were kissing again, the heat between them warming him in a whole new and delicious way. Suddenly, she pulled away. Tommy's heartbeat pounded in his ears.

"You know what? Most of all, thank you for this, right here." Then she crushed her mouth to his and he had to stop smiling to kiss her back.

Chapter Thirteen

Two days later, Pearl knocked on June's front door. As soon as it swung open, June said, "Trade you?" and handed over the fussing baby in exchange for the coffee carrier Pearl held. "Oh, sure. He immediately settles down for you. And here I am, *sweating* trying to get him to stop crying."

Pearl offered what she hoped was a reassuring smile. "This is all normal. Trust me. I know from experience. If I'd been thinking, I would have brought you an herbal iced tea instead of a hot one."

"Let me just turn on the air conditioning. I'll be right as rain." From down the hall she called, "Sterling's gonna love our electric bill this month. Nothing like running the AC in December. At least we're saving on heat since we have a wood-burning stove."

"Are you sure you want to talk about work? You seem a bit frazzled. We can just relax. I can figure out the Peaceful Pines party on my own."

When June rushed back into the living room, Pearl noticed her cheeks were rosy and strands of hair were stuck to her face. But she waved her off. "No, no. Actually, I have something to run by you. And talking about work will be a good distraction. For real. I might actually be able to concentrate because Remington isn't crying."

"Okay. If you're sure."

"I'm sure." June gave a single, decisive nod.

"Want me to pour your tea over ice for you?"

She laughed. "This is insane. Yes, please."

A few minutes later, they settled at the dining room table, Remington tucked into Pearl's left arm, June fanning herself with a folded-up new-mom pamphlet from the hospital, and the holiday party master list on the table between them.

"It looks like you've checked off the most important items," June said. "The catering and DJ are set up, the playlist is almost complete —maybe get a dozen or so more songs, so we don't have repeats if the party runs long—and you've verified all the tables and chairs. Those are really the most important items."

Pearl nodded and pointed at a few others. "I've still got to confirm the tablecloth order and make the snowflakes and center-pieces. And then there's the little matter of the resident who threat-ened to blacklist me in Prescott if I don't spike the punch."

"Let me guess: Rosa." June's voice bordered on a hysteric squeal, and Pearl laughed. "Yes. How'd you know?"

"She just has that look about her."

"Like she'd kill you as soon as she'd kill a mosquito?"

"Yes!" June covered her mouth with one hand.

"It's not funny, June! I can't spike the punch. And if I don't, she'll tell everyone I had to take over for you and the party was terrible."

June's only response was more laughter, and Pearl couldn't help but join in.

Finally, June calmed herself enough to squeak, "She won't. I mean, she might." High-pitched laughter. "But everyone will know it's not true."

"Will they?"

"They will." She cleared her throat. "So what's your plan for making the snowflakes and centerpieces? I don't think I have to point out that you don't have too much time. I mean, you could probably cut down on the volume—"

"No." Pearl held up a hand. "I'll do them all. I'll just make them when the boys are in bed."

"Not if Tommy Rowland keeps staying over after bedtime."

Pearl's face flushed, fast and hot. "How did you know?"

"Aha! You confirmed my suspicion."

Pearl gave her a dubious look, and she laughed again. "Okay, I'm lying."

"I knew it."

"Cash was patrolling over there last night and saw Tommy's car. He told Sterling, and Sterling told me."

Another dubious look, although Tommy had stayed late the night before, and they'd enjoyed a lovely second round of making out after the kids went to bed. Her mind immediately produced images of his mouth on hers, his hands gliding up her torso, hers on his—

"Okay, fine. He and Sterling were on the phone, and I heard Sterling's response, and I forced him to tell me."

"This really *is* a small town. I was in such a cocoon when I was married, I forgot just how small." The baby stirred, and she put her attention on him. "The gossip mill is real, little guy. Just you wait and see."

"More importantly, what were you guys doin' until eleven p.m.?" June sipped her tea and blinked at Pearl, all innocence.

"Gosh, it's still hot in here. Maybe I need to pour my coffee over ice, too."

"You guys were spending some alone time together after the kids went to bed, weren't you?"

"Do you remember I'm here on business?" Pearl pointed at the party-related paperwork on the table.

June waved one hand. "Yeah, but business is so *boring*."

"That's not what you thought when you rolled into town and used your business skills to save the Sweet Springs Ranch."

"Yeah, but that was before you and Tommy had a fledgling romance."

"Can we talk about snowflakes and centerpieces?"

"Fine." June's eyes were bright over the rim of her glass. "And then we're talking about you and Tommy."

"Fine." Not that she minded too much—the whole thing with

Tommy made her giddy, like a teenager, and she wanted to talk about it. "We have one week until the party. I was thinking, maybe we should add something fun for them to do. An activity of some kind."

June nodded, her eyes narrowed as she thought. "Karaoke? Christmas bingo?" She tapped her pointer finger on her chin. "White elephant?"

"Actually." Pearl cleared her throat and chastised herself for being nervous. "I saw this really cute photo booth. It's a tiny camping trailer, and they customize the inside and the props for whatever event you're doing. I know it's only a week out, but I left the tab open on my laptop and—"

"You're a genius." June lifted her glass for a toast. "This is a fantastic idea. Show me." She slid her laptop across the table and opened it. "What's it called?"

Pearl told her and she typed it in, then looked at Pearl, eyes and smile wide with excitement. "This is perfect! Let's get the okay from Marge and book it."

Pride welled in Pearl's chest. "Okay! I'll do that as soon as I get home. Didn't you say you had something else to run by me."

"Oh! Right." She pressed a palm to her forehead. "I almost forgot. You can totally say no. This is so last-minute, but it's for a friend, so I figured it wouldn't hurt to ask. You said you wanted practice, and I figured maybe Tommy could help you with the kids. It's no big deal if you don't want to—"

"June! Just tell me what it is!"

"Right. Sorry." She inhaled, and her next words came out in a fast stream: "You know Callie Walker, my sister-in-law—Hayes's wife?"

"Of course."

"Well, she decided last-minute that she wants to throw her kid's birthday party—she's turning one, so it's a big deal—the day before the Peaceful Pines party. She works full-time, you know, as an attorney, and she doesn't have time to plan it. She's not picky—"

"I'll do it." Certainty, a burning-hot flame, lit up inside Pearl.

Two parties in the same week? If they went well, she'd write her own ticket.

"You will? Are you sure? Pearl, this is a lot with the Peaceful Pines party."

"I'm sure." Imagine—if she pulled this off, she could do so much for the boys. She envisioned new soccer cleats for Wyatt and horseback riding lessons for Will. Maybe a beach vacation. She nodded. "I'll do it. Give me her contact info and I'll reach out. It's officially off your plate. In fact, I'll call her right now."

"Why don't we do a group call? I'll put her on speaker."

Callie picked up on the first ring. "Junie! How're you holding up, babe?"

"I'm great," June said. "I've got Pearl here with me, and she's a bonafide baby whisperer."

"That's wonderful," Callie said. "I wish I'd had a baby whisperer when Isla was born."

"It's really nice. But that's not what I'm calling about. I asked Pearl about the party, and—"

"I know it's a lot—"

"She said she'll do it."

Callie's elated whoops came through June's phone speaker and Pearl smiled. "Thank you so much, Pearl! You're the best. I feel so guilty I didn't think of this earlier. I mean, I *thought* of it. But her birthday just snuck up on me, and now everybody's like, 'Aren't you going to have a big party for her?' I wasn't, because she's a baby and she has no idea, but now I feel like I have to."

While Callie spoke, rapid-fire, June grinned at Pearl. They'd been friends since they were kids, and Pearl could see the love shining in June's eyes. She'd let lots of her friendships lapse when she was married to Leslie—he didn't like her going out, even for coffee or lunch, and he definitely didn't like feeling like her friendships interfered with the amount of attention Pearl could spend on him.

She resolved then and there to open herself up to new relationships, romantic and otherwise.

After a few more minutes, during which Callie explained she'd like a cowgirl-themed party for little Isla, they scheduled a meeting for the next day and hung up.

Pearl handed over the baby and left to pick up the boys, who'd persuaded Tommy he should come over right after school to help them decorate the yard. Several of their neighbors had put up illuminated deer and inflatable snowmen and tons of lights and of course Wyatt and Will wanted all of that, too.

"Where's Mr. Tommy?" Will demanded as soon as he got in the car.

"I'm glad you're so happy to see me." Pearl winked at him in the rearview mirror.

"I am happy to see you, Mama. It's just that I got used to Mr. Tommy picking us up."

"Already?"

"Already! He even gives us a special handshake when we get in the car."

Pearl's heart melted and she wondered if she was losing it. "He does?"

"Yeah. Wanna see it?" He held out his hand to demonstrate, and moved Pearl's through the motions, sliding, high-fiving, fist bumping. Pearl couldn't help but laugh while also falling for Tommy just a little bit more.

When they'd completed the handshake, Pearl said, "Well, you might be in luck. Aunt Opal's sister-in-law, Callie, asked me to plan her baby's birthday party. Which means I have a little more work. And I was thinking of—"

"Asking Mr. Tommy to pick us up more often?!"

Will's arrival coincided with Wyatt's exclamation, and Will hollered in glee. "Mr. Tommy's gonna pick us up again?"

"Sheesh. What am I, chopped liver?"

"No, it's just that Mr. Tommy is *fun*." Wyatt noticed the implication right away and his eyes went round with guilt.

Will didn't notice, and plowed on. "He plays with us and stuff."

"I play with you." Did she? Looking back on the past several weeks, Pearl realized that maybe she didn't. She'd been so busy trying to make herself indispensable to June (only so she could provide for the boys, but still).

"Not in a while." Wyatt grimaced, and her heart squeezed at the fact that he recognized he might be saying something hurtful. His next words came out in a rush. "We understand, Mama. You're working hard so you can become part of June's team and make more money and buy us lots of cool stuff." He winked.

"Yeah, Mom. We understand. It doesn't hurt our feelings. But Mr. Tommy plays with us and it's fun." Will shrugged as if that settled things.

She should have been grateful her boys had someone in their lives they considered fun. Someone who wanted to play with them, and who made up after-school handshakes with them, and who enjoyed them. She was grateful. Even so, fear prickled along the back of her neck, up onto her scalp. This situation with Tommy—this unofficial arrangement—couldn't last. It was temporary. He had to go back to work, and when he did, he wouldn't want to hang out with a couple of kids.

And what if things ended between Tommy and her? The boys would be devastated.

A relationship with him was the last thing any of them needed—so why did she want it so much?

Chapter Fourteen

Since that kiss with Pearl, Tommy couldn't think about anything else. No matter what he was doing, he was simultaneously reliving those moments. Target practice? Kissing. Cooking? Kissing. Driving? Kissing.

Sleeping? He wasn't sleeping. He was fantasizing.

Not seeing her the next day had nearly killed him, and he'd spent hours trying to think of an excuse to drop by (while imagining kissing her). Now it was the day after the day after, and he was due to go to her house because he'd promised the boys he'd help them decorate the yard.

He regretted his offer, not because he didn't want to hang out with Wyatt and Will, but because he wanted to kiss Pearl again even more, and he knew that urge would only become more intense when he saw her in person.

Two nights before as they'd dug into the casserole (before he and Pearl had shared that earth-shattering make-out session), Wyatt told him they needed a couple of new extension cords.

"Mr. Wallace's dog chewed through one, and Will cut the other one with scissors to see if he'd get electrocuted."

"Did he?" Tommy wanted to know, and Pearl threw him a dark look even as she tried not to smile.

"No." Both boys answered at the same time and then cracked up —at the dangerous situation or their own unison, Tommy didn't know.

So, Tommy made a stop at the hardware store on his way through town. A huge inflatable chimney, complete with a six-foot-tall Santa, took center stage inside. Smiling like a little kid himself, Tommy grabbed one and tossed the box into his cart before finding the outdoor extension cords.

The kids would love it. And, who was he kidding? He hoped Pearl would love it, too.

Wyatt and Will were waiting for him in the front yard when he pulled up. At the sight of his truck, they jumped around, arms in the air, cheering, and they ran to greet him once he'd parked, firing questions at him: "Did you get the extension cords?" "Will they be long enough?" "Can we plug in lights *and* the snowman?" "Can you stay for dinner again?"

"Quite a welcome you're getting, isn't it?" Pearl's voice broke through the din and Tommy paused his unloading of the truck to look at her. She stood in the doorway, arms crossed, amusement playing on her lips and in her eyes.

His body paused in response to seeing her, as if every fiber of his being wanted to absorb every detail of the moment. He shouldn't be noticing—not with her children standing just feet from him—but he couldn't help himself. Her crossed arms pushed her breasts upward, making them swell above the V of her sweater's neckline. Immediately, the memory of the weight of those breasts in his palms hit him, and he felt himself throb in response. Only then did he realize how much time had passed since she spoke. He was staring, and the additional amusement in her expression proved she'd noticed.

Which might not be a bad thing.

He just grinned at her and let his gaze skim down to her cleavage, which made her blush. "Quite a welcome."

She dropped her arms, cleared her throat, and lifted her chin toward the kids. "You've got a crew there. You put them to work in a fraction of the time it takes me to get them to do their chores. You're going to have to share all your secrets."

He narrowed his eyes at her. "I'd love to share all my secrets."

Shaking her head, still smiling, she said, "I'll leave you guys to it. I've got snowflakes to make."

"Okay." Tommy winked at her, making her blush even more fiercely before she turned around and went back inside, closing the door behind her.

"Mr. Tommy, what's this box?" Will held up the chimney-and-Santa box, hope in his eyes.

"Oh, just a little decoration I bought."

"For your house?"

"For *your* house."

Will's eyes went round. "Really?"

Tommy shrugged. "Yeah. I thought it was cool. Wait 'til you see how big it is."

Will whooped and ran off to show his brother, who whooped before running up to throw his arms around Tommy's waist. It took only about thirty minutes to get all the decorations set up, and then another hour to string the lights along the eaves, Tommy on the ladder, the boys holding the lights for him. The sun was just setting when Tommy folded the ladder and the boys ran inside to get their mom.

Tommy sent them to stand on the sidewalk where they'd have a good view, and they counted down for him to plug in the extension cords.

A cheer went up and his heart swelled as Pearl, Wyatt, and Will stared up at the house, the perfect picture of Christmas magic shining in their eyes. His entire being ached with a whole new feeling—an intensity of emotion he'd never experienced in his life.

Before he could contemplate it for too long, the three of them were walking toward him, smiling, and Wyatt was saying, "You're staying for dinner, right, Mr. Tommy?"

He looked at Pearl, and she shrugged, her face reflecting the feeling rising in his chest. "That's your invite."

"I accept."

They stood there smiling at each other for way too long.

"Are we going in?" Will asked. He tugged on Pearl's hand, and she jumped into action. "We are. Let's go."

They trooped in and the boys went to wash their hands. Tommy followed Pearl into the kitchen, where she went to the sink to wash her hands, too. He stood next to her, relishing in the simple act of sharing the soap dispenser, the way she left the water running for him when she dried her hands and then handed him the towel.

She was taking a baking dish out of the oven when she said, "I think we need to talk about what happened the other night."

His stomach dropped. Despite the way she'd been looking at him all evening, her voice sounded sad, resigned. She'd liked kissing him, he knew that. He could tell in the way her body melted against his, the way she sighed when their lips met, like she'd been waiting for just that very thing.

"Okay." He sounded as uncertain, as disappointed, as he felt, and she picked up on it.

"I liked it," she said in a rush, setting down the baking dish and turning to look at him. "I really liked it."

"But."

She sighed. "But I'm not sure it's the right path for us to go down right now."

He swallowed to clear the tightening in his throat, but couldn't quite find his voice to respond.

"It's not that I don't want to." She put a hand on his arm and his body ached for her. "It's just that I'm not sure I'm ready. You're so great with the boys and they really like you."

An involuntary smile tugged at the corner of his mouth.

"I'm just afraid that they're getting attached." She took a serving spoon out of a drawer and laid it on the counter. That's when she looked at him. "I'm afraid I am, too."

"Is that a bad thing?" He sounded so desperate, and maybe he was.

Her smile was warm. "I don't know. But it scares me."

"What if we take things slow?"

The bark of laughter she issued in response surprised him. "I mean, I think you're already in pretty deep, Rowland."

Was it bad that even though she was trying to put the brakes on their relationship, he wanted to kiss her in that moment? "Maybe I like being in deep."

"This conversation just took a turn."

They were laughing when the boys came out of the hallway.

Wyatt pointed at the table, which was covered in paper snowflakes, glitter, bits of paper, and rolls of fishing line. "Uh, Mom? Where are we gonna eat?"

"I guess we're going to have to eat in the living room."

Tommy retrieved plates and carried them to the living room after Pearl dished them up, and then the four of them gathered around the coffee table, sitting on their knees.

"How was everybody's day?" Pearl glanced at each of her kids and cut into her chicken.

"My day was good," Will said. "We played kickball at recess and I kicked the ball so hard, it flew all the way to third base and hit Kaycee Brown in the face. She cried."

"Wait." Pearl paused, mid-chew. "Your day was good because the ball you kicked hit Kaycee Brown in the face and she cried?" She glanced at Tommy as if to ask, *What is wrong with this kid?*

"No, silly! My day was good and the other thing was just something that happened."

"Oh." Pearl drew out the word, and Will said, "Really, Mom! I felt bad. I walked her to the nurse's office because her nose was bleeding."

"It just keeps getting better."

"My day was good, too," Wyatt said. "We have a project coming up. We're doing a statue garden and we have to dress up like someone famous and pretend to be that person. I have to write a speech to give when someone comes up to my statue."

"Who'd you pick?" Tommy asked.

"Abraham Lincoln. Because he wore a really cool hat."

Tommy now knew where the phrase, "Kids say the darnedest things" came from. "I mean, he did some cool things back in the day, too, right?"

"Right." Wyatt's dismissive gesture made Tommy laugh out loud. "But I think he wore a coat with those long things in the back."

"Tails?" Pearl supplied.

"Yeah. Tails." He pointed at her. "How was your day, Mr. Tommy?"

It had been a long time since he'd sat around the dinner table, casual, and had someone ask how his day was. "It was good. Thanks for asking."

"What'd you do?" Will asked.

"Well, I worked on my target shooting some more, and I cleaned up around my house. I watched some TV."

Will looked at Wyatt. "Sounds kind of boring."

"Depends what you watched on TV, I guess."

"How was your day, Mama?" Will said.

Pearl sighed. "It was really good. Except I feel like I still have so much to do." She inclined her head toward the dining room table—and the snowflakes. "After I finish the snowflakes, I have to finish the centerpieces. And this seems like a good time to bring up one more thing." She grimaced at Tommy. "I already told the boys this, but Callie Wilder asked me to plan Isla's first birthday party."

"That's great news! Right? Why do you look like you regret it?"

"I don't regret it, exactly. It's just that it's going to be at almost the same time as the Peaceful Pines party. June said I didn't have to do it, but I want to. I want to help Callie, of course, and I also felt like it would make me indispensable."

Will leaned over to whisper to Wyatt. "What's indispensable?"

Wyatt whispered back. "It's, like, you can't live without her."

"You *are* indispensable, Mama!" Will piped up.

"Aw, thanks, sweetie. But I need to be indispensable to June, too, so she lets me keep working with her. And it all starts with these snowflakes."

"We'll help you, Mama!" Will jumped up from his spot at the coffee table, leaving his plate there when he rushed to the dining room.

"Aw, thank you," Pearl said. "But take your plate to the kitchen first, okay?"

"Mr. Tommy, are you gonna help, too?"

Tommy looked at Pearl, who said, "You don't have to."

"I'll stay." He did his best to act nonchalant even though his heart was dancing around inside his ribcage at the prospect of spending more time with her.

They cleaned up from dinner, the kids once again pitching in and Pearl raising an eyebrow at Tommy as they worked together to load the dishwasher. Then they all gathered around the dining room table to make snowflakes. While they cut and glued and glittered and tied, they chatted about the day, movies they'd watched, and their plans for the weekend.

Pearl gasped when she looked at her watch. "Boys! It's bedtime!"

Two sets of shoulders slumped, making Tommy laugh again, even though he could empathize with their disappointment that the evening was coming to an end.

"Wow, I think we must have made about a hundred snowflakes, though! Thank you guys, so much, for your help. We have only about a million more to do!"

"A million?" Will's eyebrows shot up.

"I was just kidding. About a hundred more."

"We just need one more work session," Wyatt said. "Are you in, Mr. Tommy?"

"I'm here for it." Tommy couldn't believe a couple of hours had passed before he even had a chance to think about the time. "But only if you guys get ready for bed right away. If we're not careful, your mom will think that the excitement of me being here is keeping you awake. Because we all know how exciting I am."

The boys were in stitches at that, but they did get up and go into the bathroom without another word.

"Thank you for your help." Pearl stood up and started organizing the completed snowflakes and all the supplies. "The three of you really sped up the process."

"You're welcome."

"Listen—"

"Wait." Tommy held up a hand. "Can I just say one thing? I

don't want you to think I didn't hear what you said earlier. About you not being sure if you're ready for a relationship. Trust me, the last thing I want to do is pressure you. But I was wondering if you'd be willing to give this—us—a chance." Her movements paused and he rushed to go on before she responded. "I really like being around you, Pearl. And the kids, too. And I can't promise things will work out, but I also don't want to pass up the chance to find out. You make me feel ... lighter, somehow. I know, that sounds cheesy. But you do, Pearl. When we're not together, I'm thinking about you. And the boys, too. But mostly you. I'm thinking about what I can do to make you smile, what I can do to make your life easier, how I can make you happy."

Somewhere during his speech, her shoulders had relaxed. She stood next to the table, her eyes on his.

"This is a first," he said. "It's never been like this for me before. And I don't know where this thing between us is going, but I'd sure like to explore it. If you're willing."

She nodded, businesslike but still a little wide-eyed, and his heart unlocked. "I'm willing." Before he could jump to his feet and hug her, she held up a hand. "But."

"Not again," he said, and she laughed.

"But. I want you to know that I'm scared. You seem really great. We seem really great, together. But there's a part of me that worries it's too good to be true. That you'll realize what you're getting into, and cut us loose. And it's not just me—it's Wyatt and Will, too."

As if to prove that point, sounds of the boys arguing came down the hallway.

"I know it is. And I don't take that lightly. The three of you are a package deal—and it's a deal I'm all in on."

Again, she nodded. Then she bent down and pressed her lips to his, briefly but firmly, and relief bloomed in his chest. "Okay. Then we'll try it. As long as you promise to let us down easy."

He shook his head. "I don't plan on letting you down."

"I know you don't." Something flashed in her eyes—pain, certainly, but it was mixed with something else. Regret, maybe? Memories?

"If we're going to try this, I want you to go on a date with me."

Her expression shifted, relaxed, and she smiled. "Deal."

She kissed him again, and he knew his heart would break if she changed her mind.

Chapter Fifteen

A date. How long had it been since Pearl went on an actual date?

Here she was, on a Friday night, having dropped the kids off with Opal and Cash. She stood in her bedroom, preparing to go out with a man other than her ex-husband. Her first first date in more than a decade and a half. If she hadn't already spent so much time with Tommy, she'd be nervous.

She laughed out loud at that thought. "Who am I kidding? I'm as nervous as I've ever been."

It was only natural to think back on the beginning of her relationship with Leslie. They met on a warm fall day during their first semester of college at Central Arizona University. During a break between her biology and English classes, Pearl found a sunny spot to read. After a few minutes, a shadow loomed over her, blocking the sun and its warmth. She looked up, hoping the shadow belonged to one of the girlfriends she'd made.

But no, it belonged to a very tall, very handsome young man with very broad shoulders. Her first thought was that his silhouette looked like those of many of the cartoon heroes she'd seen in the movies of her childhood. She had to squint to make out his features, and they matched the look she'd started to envision: thick brows on a prominent brow line, a nice, strong chin, and dark green eyes.

"This is far too nice a day to be reading," he'd said. That should have been her first clue they weren't meant for each other. The day was perfect for reading outside in the warm, fresh air. But, smitten with his smile and bravado, she accepted his invitation when he asked if he could take her out.

For the rest of the week, she agonized over what to wear, asking her roommates for their opinions and even searching the Internet for *what to wear on a first date* and *best outfits to impress a new boyfriend* and *most flattering outfits for romance*. All she cared about was whether she'd impress him, whether she'd be enough.

Leslie picked her up in his father's fancy convertible sports car and drove her to a swanky club. The sign on the door said you had to be twenty-one to get in, but he exchanged a look with the bouncer and they slid past the velvet rope and through the velvet curtains and into a dark room crowded with gyrating bodies. He bought her a drink and they found a booth, where they sat sipping from their crystal glasses, unable to talk to each other over the deafening music.

Then they danced. And oh, was he a good dancer. His skills on that dance floor won her over so fast, she didn't even have time to realize he wasn't right for her before she fell headlong in love with him.

But, modern-day Pearl thought, this was different. Here she was, a full-on adult who had spent the last year getting to really know herself again. A grown woman who was pulling on her sexiest, laciest thong and matching bra, not because she wanted to impress Tommy (although that would be a bonus), but because she *wanted* him, because his hands on her body turned her on, because she craved being close to him, and this underwear made her feel sexy as hell.

She was nervous, but it was a different kind of nervous. She wasn't worried about whether she would impress Tommy, or be enough for him. She was worried that she'd fall hard for him and later discover they weren't right for each other.

And that would hurt.

God, how that realization had hurt her when she experienced it with Leslie. She couldn't go through that again. She had to make sure she and Tommy were right for each other before her feelings were too strong.

Is it too late? Well, even if it was, she'd enjoy it tonight.

She pulled on her best-fitting black pants, slim to the ankles and very flattering on her backside, according to Opal, and then her softest sweater, hoping it would tell Tommy, *Look how touchable I am.*

He got the message. When she opened the door he gave her a once-over that said he was hungry, starving, famished, actually, and then he stepped close to her, ran his hands up her arms and down her back before pulling her in for a long, slow kiss. The door stood open, and there was something magical about kissing this man in the glow of the lights from the Christmas decorations he'd helped put up.

If music had been playing, it would have ground to a halt a second later when he straightened up and said, "Wait. The boys are gone, right?"

She laughed, grateful for the momentary release of tension. "Right. I took them to Opal and Cash's so I could get ready in peace."

His eyes soft, he said, "You look beautiful."

He couldn't have chosen a better word. "Thank you."

"Shall we?" He offered his arm and they stepped out into the crisp December air, which made her gasp. "I haven't been outside the house today, except to the garage and in the car. It's so much colder than it was yesterday."

"I know. It's freezing. I hope it doesn't ruin my plans, but if there's anything you don't want to do, just say so."

Intrigued and hoping for more information, Pearl looked up at him, but he just grinned and opened the passenger door of his truck. He offered his hand to help her climb in. While she waited for him to walk around to the driver's side, she noticed the pine-and-wood scent of the air freshener. How strange it was to sit in a man's truck, to occupy this space. It felt so intimate all of a sudden. Panic rose and her heart raced. Was she really ready for dating? But then Tommy got in the car, picked up his phone, and asked her what music she wanted to listen to. The task of choosing something forced her to focus and cooled the emotional uprising.

Scrolling through his music app was enlightening. His "recently played" section included a good variety: country, rock, a couple of movie soundtracks, even classical.

"Wow, you've got quite the diverse library here."

He put the truck in reverse and backed out of the driveway. "I like different things, depending on my mood."

"Me, too."

"What're you in the mood for now?"

Something in his voice had her saying to herself, *You're talking about music, Pearl.*

"Will you be disappointed if I say not Christmas music?"

He laughed. "Nope. Still working on that playlist?"

"Yep. I love Christmas music in general, but I've heard Mariah Carey and Michael Bublé about a thousand times a day."

She ended up picking a rock station, and he drummed his thumbs on the steering wheel as he drove. Was he nervous? That idea melted her heart, and she decided she'd be less nervous if she tried to put him at ease."So where are we going, anyway?"

"I was originally thinking Art Deco, but, ah—my sources suggested something different."

"You asked Opal."

"I did."

"That is so cute."

"It is? I was afraid you'd think it was unoriginal, that I lacked creativity."

She laughed. "Not at all. You've got my sister at your disposal—I'm glad you used her. I think it's resourceful."

His grip on the steering wheel relaxed.

"So, where are we going?"

"I wanted to take you somewhere quiet and relaxing, but not stuffy."

"Okay." She drew the word out, waiting.

"Someplace where you could just relax." He glanced at her. Licked his lips. He *was* nervous.

She put a hand on his arm. "That sounds lovely."

"It might be different from what you're thinking."

"I'm sure it'll be perfect."

And it was. Tommy drove them downtown, where multi-colored Christmas lights adorned the stately old courthouse building and shone from the giant trees lining the quaint square. After parking, he led Pearl down the sidewalk to the Rusty Spur. Although the sign on the door read *Closed*, the garland around the door twinkled with an illuminated wreath, and the restaurant's inside lights were on.

"Wait. I thought they only served breakfast and lunch."

"They do." He pulled open the door and stood back to let her enter before him. "And tonight, they're serving breakfast for dinner—just for the two of us."

Her mouth dropped open and her heart practically exploded with gratitude as she walked into the warmth of the restaurant and inhaled the scents of maple syrup and bread baking. "They are?!"

"Yeah." After a brief moment, concern replaced his satisfied smile. "Wait. Is that a good 'They are,' or a bad 'They are'?"

The door closed behind them.

"It's a good one. A great one." She wrapped her arms around his waist and squeezed. "This might just be the most thoughtful thing anyone has done for me."

He glowed at the compliment.

"Do you know how much I love breakfast food?"

"A couple of little birdies might have mentioned it."

She raised an eyebrow and he elaborated.

"The first day I babysat them, Wyatt and Will quizzed me on all my favorites—food, color, music, car, season, day of the week." He shrugged. "And is it a crime that I used that conversation to get a little dirt on you, too?"

"Good evening." A man walked into the dining room from the kitchen, smiling broadly.

"Hey, Mr. Slade." Tommy and Mr. Slade shook hands. "This is Pearl Houston."

"Pleasure to make your acquaintance." Mr. Slade's eyes crinkled at the corners as he smiled and grasped Pearl's hand.

"Likewise. Are you really opening up this evening just for us?"

"I am. It so happens, I owe Mr. Rowland here a big favor. After tonight, though, we'll be even." He winked at Tommy. "Sit anywhere you like."

Again, Tommy gestured for Pearl to go ahead, and she chose a cozy corner booth.

Mr. Slade declared it a "great choice," handed them menus once they were seated, and told them he'd be back to take their orders.

When they were alone, Pearl reached across the table to take Tommy's hand. "This is incredible. Really."

"I'm so glad you think so. It was a risk."

Mr. Slade returned with a tray bearing a carafe of orange juice, a bottle of champagne, and two champagne flutes. Pearl beamed at Tommy. "Mimosas in the evening?"

"Absolutely."

Mr. Slade set down all the supplies. "I'll let you guys decide how strong to make 'em. Have you had a chance to look at the menu?"

They ordered a smorgasbord of breakfast foods—an omelette, blueberry pancakes, hash browns, biscuits and gravy, and muffins— and Mr. Slade didn't bat an eye as he wrote it all down and went back into the kitchen.

"Mimosa?" Tommy held up the orange juice carafe.

"Yes, please."

He poured two, handed her a glass, and held his up. "To our first date."

"Cheers."

They drank and Pearl would have sworn she could feel the effects of the champagne right away."I'm so impressed you pulled this off."

"What can I say? I'm an impressive guy."

"You are." Again, she felt the urge to touch him, and she didn't resist. She reached across the table and intertwined her fingers with his. "This is really special."

"You're welcome. *You're* really special."

Mr. Slade returned with the omelette. "I figured I'd serve you in courses. If I bring it all at once, you won't be able to taste everything."

Over the next two hours, they sipped their mimosas, ate their giant feast, and talked. They discussed their childhoods, their current jobs, and their favorite seasons. He asked about her dream vacation and she asked about the best book he'd ever read. She told him about the last TV series she'd watched—a docuseries about unsolved murders—and he told her about playing in a darts tournament with the Wilder brothers.

At one point, he looked at his watch and said, "I may have planned differently if I'd known we'd talk for so long, but we've got to go."

"Where are we going?"

His eyes lit up. "It's a surprise. Let's get some boxes. It's so cold, the leftovers will keep if we leave them in the truck."

A few minutes later, they'd put the takeout boxes in the backseat and Tommy was leading Pearl down the sidewalk again—this time, to the opposite corner of the courthouse plaza. The nighttime air chilled her cheeks as they walked, and when he said, "We're here," she gasped at what stood in front of them.

An ornate horse-drawn carriage and four Clydesdales waited along the curb, and a driver—wearing a top hat and a vintage velvet coat, raised his hand in greeting when they approached.

"Are we going for a ride?" Her voice held all the wonder she felt.

"We are."

She actually squealed and found herself hugging him again. "I cannot believe it. Do you know how much I've always wanted to do this?"

The rumble of laughter in his chest vibrated against her ear and she felt a bolt of heat shoot straight through her core and land between her legs.

"I didn't know that, but I had a feeling you'd like it. Are you ready?"

"*So* ready."

The driver helped Pearl into the carriage first, and she settled into the leather seat while Tommy climbed in. Just as she wondered how cold it'd be as they drove around, the driver opened a trunk attached to the side of the carriage and pulled out a blanket, which he handed to them. They unfolded it and spread it over their laps. Its weight and thickness immediately warmed Pearl's body.

"Shall we?" The driver looked up at them, they gave him a thumbs up, and he climbed up onto the bench at the front of the carriage. He clicked his tongue and, harnesses creaking, the horses began to move.

Giddy, Pearl pulled the blanket up to her chin and snuggled against Tommy. "This is so romantic."

He rested his cheek on the top of her head. "It is, isn't it?"

"Certainly the most romantic date I've ever been on."

"That's what I was going for." Under the blanket, his hand found hers and wrapped around it. "I wanted tonight to be special."

She sighed. "It is. This is a whole new way to experience the Christmas lights." Faster than walking, slower than driving, and so old-fashioned in the best possible way, so classical, so *pure*. Exactly like Tommy. He'd been nothing but the perfect gentleman, his affection for her undiluted. "It's perfect."

Tiny, swirling snowflakes started to fall then, dancing in the ambient light, landing gentle and silent on the blanket, in Pearl's hair, on the horses' backs, and on the driver's shoulders. Pearl tilted her head back and felt the icy sprinkles on her face.

"Would the lovely couple like to end the ride early, or carry on?" The driver had turned around in his seat. "The horses don't mind either way. In fact, I think they rather enjoy the snowfall."

Tommy looked at Pearl. "What do you think?"

"I'd love to finish the ride. But only if it's okay with the horses."

The driver chuckled. "Trust me, darlin'. They'd let us know if it wasn't. They'd be booking it for the trailer the next block over."

So they carried on, the carriage wheels creaking quietly as they rolled along under the Christmas lights, the snow sparkling and magical all around them.

* * *

They hadn't planned on Tommy spending the night, but after that magical, snowy carriage ride, one thing led to another and she was pulling him into the house and they were kissing in front of the Christmas tree and it was after midnight and she found herself asking him to stay.

The fact that she asked while their lips were still touching probably implied that she wanted him to *stay* stay, and when he asked if she was sure, she responded by unbuckling his belt.

She wanted this, wanted him, and silenced the voice in the back of her mind that threw out so many questions: *Are you sure about this, Pearl? How long has it been? Will it be weird having sex with someone new?*

It wasn't weird.

It was gentle and passionate and tender and so very lovely.

When she would have stripped him down right there in the living room, he led her to the bedroom and slowly, slowly peeled off her sweater, taking his time to lavish each breast before moving on to her pants and her lower belly and God, she couldn't remember the last time someone had taken such care with her.

In turn, she, too, took her time exploring his body—the smoothness of his chest and the ridges of his abs and the firmness of his butt.

The experience of starting anew with someone, getting to know his body, was so delicious, she nearly cried when he laid her down on the bed and stretched his body alongside hers. His fingertips trailed over her skin—her arms, chest, breasts, and stomach, and she slid her legs along his until she was nearly ready to come undone.

"I want you inside me." She registered briefly that she sounded quite like a vixen.

"Are you sure?"

Their eyes met, and the flame of desire between her legs only flared up, forcing her to move against him.

"*So* sure."

He entered her then, so slowly, she ached as she pressed against him. "Okay?"

"More than okay." She kissed him. "Really, really good."

Smiling, he pulled out and entered her again, then made long, slow strokes, driving her higher and higher. Just as she neared the edge, he went deep and then stopped. When she opened her eyes, she found that he was looking at her, intense.

"Are you okay?" She hoped he was. She was desperate for him to be okay.

He nodded. "I just wanted to tell you—I don't do this all the time. This is special to me. You're special to me."

Her entire being expanded in that moment, his heartfelt words reaching deep into her core. She felt herself smile, the unrestrained smile of true joy, and she said, "Thank you for saying that. I hope you know it's the same for me. You're really special to me, too, and not just because you fix my appliances and babysit my children."

His eyes were smiling when he said, "Did you have to talk about the kids?"

"Let's just get back to what we were doing."

He throbbed inside her and they started moving together again, the mood transforming from slow and sweet to fast and fevered, and they both toppled over the edge together.

After she retrieved a towel and they cleaned up, they climbed under the covers together. Her body pliable and deeply relaxed, Pearl fell asleep immediately.

Chapter Sixteen

Tommy woke up the next morning to the deep silence of a snow day and the deep comfort of a woman in his arms. Not just any woman, but Pearl. *The woman.* That thought startled him. The light coming through the window was blinding white—proof, in addition to the blanketing silence—that lots of snow had fallen overnight.

After I made love to Pearl like I've never made love to anyone else.

He'd really enjoy waking her up with another round of said lovemaking, but he had to use the bathroom. And ... the kids. Pearl had asked Opal to keep them overnight and said she'd pick them up first thing in the morning.

Only, they were all snowed in and the roads probably weren't even clear yet. Tommy eased his arm out from under Pearl's body and slipped out of bed. The house was cold and he felt goosebumps rise on his skin as he walked to the bathroom.

Before returning to the warmth of the bed, he made a quick detour to look out the living room window at the street. Sure enough, the drifts were waist-high. A shiver of anticipation ran through him. Opal and Cash lived at a slightly higher elevation and just out of town, which meant they probably had slightly more snow and their roads would be plowed slightly later.

Which meant he and Pearl had some time.

His body already showing signs of arousal, he hurried back to the bedroom. How a woman could stop him in his tracks—simply by looking at him from bed, her hair fanned around her head—he'd never know. But she did. He froze, mid-stride, and she smiled, which took his breath away.

"You're awake."

"I am. And I'm hoping you're coming back to bed."

"It snowed." He walked toward the bed, slowly, predatory.

"I see that."

"The road hasn't been plowed."

"Which means Opal and Cash's definitely hasn't been plowed."

"Right."

"Which means we can't get there to get the kids, and they can't get here to bring the kids." Her smile had turned wicked.

"Exactly."

"Which means we have time."

"That's what I was thinking."

Her arms encircled his neck. Her lips touched his. She pulled back the covers to invite him in. When he saw that she was naked—they'd both put on t-shirts the night before—he went hard instantly and slid into the bed next to her, letting his skin move against hers. Again, their bodies moved together and Tommy could swear their souls had known each other forever or maybe longer.

They spent the morning in bed, except when they got up to make breakfast and coffee, which they brought back to bed. Pearl texted Opal, who sent back pictures of the boys making snowmen and snow angels and bounding through the snow with the dog, Louie.

As Tommy expected, Cash and Opal had gotten even more snow than Pearl had, and they figured it'd be a while until the snowplows came. So while Opal and Cash enjoyed Wyatt and Will, Tommy enjoyed Pearl. They talked and laughed and kissed and made love, and he couldn't remember ever feeling the way he did for her.

Finally, by late afternoon, the sun came out and melted the snow off the roads, and before long, Cash's truck came rumbling down the street. He pulled into the driveway and cut the engine, and the sounds of rowdy boys replaced the diesel purr.

Tommy and Pearl had talked about whether he should go home before the boys came back and ultimately decided he wouldn't—they could just tell the boys he'd come over to shovel the driveway.

"You should stay," Pearl said. "They'll be so excited to tell you all about the snow day, anyway." That gave Tommy all these warm and fuzzy feelings to which he wasn't accustomed, and he agreed.

To his surprise, Wyatt and Will didn't seem to register his presence as abnormal (cue even more warm, fuzzy feelings). They came tearing up the walkway, talking a mile a minute, sharing all the stories from the morning.

Pearl offered to make everyone hot chocolate, and the women and kids disappeared into the house, leaving Tommy outside with Cash.

"Did you plan that snow day, or something? Call in a favor with the weather gods?"

Tommy laughed and felt the heat rush to his face. "No. That'd be cool, but it was just Christmas luck, I guess."

"I don't think I have to ask if the date went well."

If it were possible, he blushed even more fiercely. "I'd say the evidence points to it going well."

"I heard you rented a horse-drawn carriage."

"Word travels fast." Not that he'd wanted to keep it a secret, but he didn't know if he was ready for his friend to know just how smitten he was with Pearl.

"Pretty fancy, bro." Cash wiggled his eyebrows.

A gust of cold wind came through, brushing over Tommy's neck, making him shiver. He shrugged. "I thought it would be a nice way to see the Christmas lights. And then it snowed, and that was pretty awesome."

"And then what?" Cash used his foot to push a small pile of

snow off the walkway, and then broke a thin sheet of ice with his heel.

"And then we went home."

"And?" Cash looked at him, his eyes piercing.

"Getting kind of nosy, there, aren't you?" He was blushing so hard, his eyes were watering.

Cash slapped him on the back. "I'm just messing with you, man. I'm glad you guys had a good night. We had fun with the kids."

"They're good kids."

"They are. You almost can't help but get attached to the whole bunch, right?"

Tommy nodded. "Right."

"What's going to happen when you go back to work?"

"I don't know." He ran a hand across the back of his neck—a nervous gesture he was sure Cash recognized.

"You've thought about it?"

"I really like her." He hoped his look was piercing enough for Cash to know he was serious.

"I know. She's great. But she's also been through a lot. I guess I just wanted to make sure you're still going to really like her once you go back to work and no longer need the distraction."

Anger flared in Tommy's chest, molten, and he clenched his fists. Which was weird, because he genuinely *liked* Cash. They'd become close when Tommy was Cash's field training officer, and even closer as they'd worked the same shift over the past year. Not once in all that time had Tommy wanted to punch Cash in the kisser like he did at the moment.

Cash had once told him how hard he worked on practicing his observation skills, per the instructions of Commander Mosley in the police academy. Those skills must have been sharp, because Cash's gaze dropped to Tommy's fists and he grinned. "Okay, man. I see I struck a nerve, which tells me everything I need to know."

Tommy growled—actually growled, like some kind of animal.

Cash had the nerve to laugh. "Sheesh. You know, she's my sister-in-law. I'm sort of obligated to look out for her. It's nothing personal."

"The hell it's not."

"Wait." Cash's eyes went round. "Are you in love with her, Rowland?"

Tommy cursed his pale complexion and the reddening of his neck and cheeks, yet again. *Am I?*

"I think you are, bro!"

"You think he's what?" Will had come out of the house and stood outside the front door in his bare feet.

"Nothing," Tommy said, his voice way harsher than he intended.

Will's mouth dropped open—Tommy had never spoken to him like that—and guilt immediately rushed in. Tommy ran up to him in a couple of strides and then scooped him up, tickling him. Fortunately, Will dissolved into giggles.

"What were you coming out here for, you little dragon-killing alien?"

Through fits of laughter, Will said, "I was coming to tell you the hot chocolate's ready."

Relieved the conversation with Cash was over for now, Tommy threw Will over his shoulder and headed for the front door.

Twenty minutes later, the boys had settled on the couch to watch a movie and the adults gathered by the door so Tommy and Pearl could send off Cash and Opal. Despite his reasonable side telling him Cash was just doing right by Pearl—which Tommy admired—his emotional side still felt a bit frosty toward his friend.

"How's the shooting going?" Cash's tone was casual, as if he couldn't still feel Tommy's fire burning.

"Fine." His teeth were clenched and he consciously relaxed his jaw.

"When are you going in to take the test?"

Another touchy subject. "Tomorrow."

Pearl gasped and looked at him. "Tomorrow?"

What was it about this group that was making Tommy blush on repeat? "Yeah."

"Why didn't you say anything? I wouldn't have kept you so busy."

He shrugged. "I don't know. It's not a big deal."

"The hell it's not."

He was developing a sudden and very strong dislike for Cash Wilder. "It's not, man. I've been practicing. I'll be fine."

Now, Cash shrugged, the movement ultra casual just like when he'd asked how the shooting was going. "Okay. Whatever you say."

Pearl and Opal exchanged a glance—one of those looks where two women shared an entire silent conversation—and then Opal announced that she and Cash were leaving. In the silence they left behind, Pearl grabbed Tommy's wrist. "Why didn't you tell me you were taking the test tomorrow?"

Guilt—over the hurt he'd obviously caused her—disguised itself as defensiveness, which prickled along his skin. "I don't know. Like I said, it's not that big of a deal. It's when the boys are in school, so I figured I'd just go get it done and tell you about it after."

"After you pass." She was smiling now, and he hoped they were beyond that moment.

"Exactly."

* * *

Susie, one of the police department's administrative assistants, had called Tommy to set up his testing appointment, but she hadn't known who'd oversee it. When he pulled up at the shooting range and saw Commander Mosley hoisting his giant frame out of his car, he groaned.

Mosley wasn't a bad guy, but he wasn't the sort of guy who put a person at ease, either. He'd been in charge when Tommy went through the police academy, and his appearance could silence any room before a police recruit could say "terror."

Tommy took a moment to center himself. He closed his eyes and envisioned himself holding his duty weapon, pulling the trigger in one smooth motion of his middle finger, going through the whole process with calm and precision, each bullet going straight through the center of the target.

A couple of loud raps on his window startled him out of his

meditative state, and he was eye to push-broom mustache with Mosley.

"You comin', Rowland?"

He nodded and, movements clumsy (which didn't bode well for his test), rushed to unbuckle his seatbelt. "I'm coming."

"Good. Let's get this show on the road. I haven't got all day."

With one more deep breath to fortify himself, Tommy grabbed his gun bag and got out of the car. A couple of other officers were inside, which rattled him anew. He'd been hoping he'd be alone during the test, but now he had an audience. They'd probably all be watching to see how he did. If he was enough of an idiot to lose a finger after slamming it in a car door, how would be learn to shoot with a different finger?

"Where should I set up?"

Mosley's expression told him he was also an idiot for asking. "Any open lane, Rowland."

Heart racing, hands shaking, armpits sweating, he found an empty lane, took out his gun, and put in a magazine. Mosley came to stand next to him, which took up pretty much all the available oxygen. "Ready, Rowland?"

Not even close. He nodded. "Ready."

Chapter Seventeen

Pearl sat at her desk in June's office, checking off what she hoped were the final to-do lists for Baby Isla's first birthday party and the Peaceful Pines holiday party, which were in three and four days, respectively. Her head throbbed from exhaustion—not that she'd exchange any of the moments she'd spent with Tommy for sleep—and she rubbed her temples.

She had just ten minutes of uninterrupted work time left. After that, she had to pack up and get the boys.

For about the hundredth time that day, she looked at the date. For the first time that day, she realized only one week remained until Christmas. She cursed. "Gifts." She hadn't bought a single gift for Wyatt and Will.

Not that she hadn't *thought* about what to buy them. Each one would get a new set of LEGO blocks, a couple of books, and a pair of new pajamas. Those were yearly staples. But she wanted to get them a few more things, and her brainstorming hadn't produced anything exciting ... probably because she'd been so distracted.

Not just with the event planning, but with Tommy.

Maybe Leslie, the jerk of an ex husband that he was, had been right that she couldn't parent well if she had anything else going on. That's why he hadn't "let" her get a job when they were married.

Heart racing now, she opened a new tab on her Internet browser and typed in the site for the online megastore where she usually bought gifts. The site populated results for her *LEGO sets* search, and she gasped as she saw delivery date after delivery date—a note under every item read, "Arrives after Christmas."

Pearl took a deep breath. "It's fine. I'll just go shopping in real life." She nodded, as if to confirm the legitimacy of her idea.

Only, then she remembered her to-do lists, which would have her days absolutely packed for the next several days. If she waited until after the parties, the stores would probably be stripped clean of LEGO sets and Christmas pajamas. Same with any other "cool" gifts, because all the other parents, who were surely more on top of things than she was, would have snapped up everything good. Maybe she could go late at night or early in the morning, while the kids slept. Which sounded miserable.

"What about ship to store?" Another tab, another round of bad news. *Arrives after Christmas.* She groaned. "Okay, so early-morning or late-night shopping it is."

Maybe Opal or Tommy could stay at the house while she went, just in case. She balled one hand into a fist and knocked her forehead against it. How could she have been so stupid?

Her phone rang and she nearly cried when she saw Opal's name on the screen.

"What's wrong?" Opal demanded as soon as she answered.

Pearl inhaled, taking a moment to set aside her irritation over the fact that Opal always, *always* knew when something was wrong and to instead be grateful for that. Then, in a rushed voice that bordered on blubbering, she told Opal everything. "And, as wrapped up as I was in planning the parties and dating Tommy and, let's face it, having the best sex of my life, I completely forgot to follow through and actually buy presents for my kids. And before you say presents aren't everything and Christmas isn't all about presents, let's not forget how excited we used to get to see all the presents under the tree on Christmas morning."

Opal sighed. "You're right. I was going to say that, and I was going to tell you I'm sure they appreciate everything you're doing for them—because this holiday party stuff is for them, isn't it? But you're right, they're kids. They're expecting presents. I can help you shop—"

Pearl dropped her head into her spare hand. "No, it's okay." She softened her tone. "I mean, I really appreciate it, but I feel like it won't mean as much if I send their aunt to do the shopping, as much as they love you. It's something I've got to do. I was thinking I might ask you to babysit again, though."

"You know I will. When?"

"That's the thing. I've got myself completely booked up during the reasonable hours. I might have to go while they're sleeping. I'm going to have to figure this out and let you know."

They disconnected, and Pearl's airways tightened with panic. How would she ever get all the snowflakes and centerpieces assembled? Not to mention the balloon arch for Callie's baby's first birthday party.

She groaned.

"This is impossible."

"What's impossible?" June's voice startled her.

"Hey! You're supposed to be resting." Pearl turned her computer chair around to smile at June.

"I know, but the baby's sleeping—finally—and I thought I'd come check on you, see how things are going."

Pearl warred with herself. Could she admit that she was absolutely drowning? June might know what to do, or who to call for help. But what if Pearl's confession shed light on the fact that she was, in fact, incompetent? No, she wouldn't say anything. She'd keep her problem and her stress to herself. But she had to say something. Hadn't she read something somewhere about sticking as close to the truth as possible?

"Oh, just looking at a few Christmas gifts for the boys." She turned back around to look at her computer screen. "Looks like they're not going to get here in time for Christmas if I order them online." She tapped a few keys on the keyboard and rushed to add, "Which is no biggie. I'll just hit up the stores around here." *Between snowflakes and centerpieces and a giant balloon arch.*

"You sure? I could help you."

Pearl waved her off. "Absolutely not. I appreciate it, so much, but you've got the baby to tend to. I'm sure the last thing you want is to be out in the Christmas rush with all those people and their germs."

June shrugged. "You make a good point. But let me know if there's any other way I can help. I can research online while I nurse the baby. We're obviously not getting him much this year—he won't know, and he's not even supposed to be here, yet!"

That made Pearl laugh. "He's the best gift of all, though, isn't he?"

"He is. All right. I'll leave you to it. Something tells me it's time to feed Remington." The sound of wails emanated from the baby monitor she held in one hand. Let me know if you need anything, Pearl."

And then she was gone, and Pearl decided the best course of action was to pick up the boys and then get home and pound out the snowflakes and centerpieces, and start inflating balloons.

When she pulled up at the curb at the boys' school, Wyatt looked ashen. His eyes looked huge and dark against his pale face, and a few slithering snakes took up residence in Pearl's stomach.

"Mom!" He lurched into the backseat, then put his hands on her headrest and pulled himself forward so his face was just inches from hers. "We forgot! My Abe Lincoln project is due tomorrow! I need a coat with tails and a top hat. And a beard."

"By tomorrow?"

"I told you about this, Mom. Remember? A week ago. When we were eating dinner. I told you I chose Abe Lincoln because he wore a top hat."

Pearl nodded. Swallowed. She had even less time to shop for an Abe Lincoln outfit than she did to shop for Christmas presents, and Christmas presents seemed vastly more important at the moment. To her. But judging by Wyatt's face, an Abe Lincoln costume was of the utmost importance.

"Mom! This counts for so many points. Like, if I don't do a good job on this, it'll *tank* my history grade."

Before she could even respond, Will was lurching into the car, too. "Mom! I got a bloody nose today!"

At least he didn't have a giant project due, as well.

"I'm sorry," Pearl said, and Wyatt shot, "Quit being a baby, Will. Who cares about a bloody nose? We need an Abe Lincoln costume. We're going shopping right now, right, Mom?"

"I guess we have no choice."

Stress sitting like a ball of lead in her stomach, she pulled away from the curb and almost hit a car that was passing on her left. The driver honked and she lifted an apologetic hand. "Asshole."

"Mom!" Will admonished her. "That's a bad word."

"I know."

And then they were off to the store, her visions of getting to all her craft projects dissolving.

Chapter Eighteen

Tommy couldn't believe it: he'd failed his shooting test. Sleep deprived and distracted (and who wouldn't be, with visions of his night with Pearl—her skin aglow in the moonlight—dancing in his mind's eye?), his bullet grouping had been all over the target.

He walked out of the shooting range with his shoulders slumped and his head down, not only disappointed in himself, but embarrassed beyond belief.

When he was going through the academy, his fellow recruits had called him Sharpshooter or Ace because he'd hit every target, every time. His groupings were sometimes less than an inch around —each bullet nearly passing through the hole made by the previous one. When they had to certify each year, the other guys would joke that he had to go last; no one wanted to shoot after he did, because he'd show them all up.

And then he'd gone and failed his re-certification.

He got into his truck and slammed the door so hard, the coins rattled in the center console. He swore, yanked his seatbelt across his torso, and slammed the metal tab into the buckle, then rammed the gear shift into reverse. Although the temptation to jam down the gas pedal was strong, he forced oxygen into his lungs, exhaled, and looked behind him before backing slowly out of his spot.

Anger had his blood boiling. He couldn't see straight. "I probably shouldn't be driving." The words came out through his gritted teeth.

When he'd brought the target whizzing back on the clothesline, Mosley had grabbed it in his beefy hand, jerked it off the clip, and hissed through his teeth. "This is bad, Rowland."

Tommy thought he was joking at first. But when Mosley looked at him, eyebrows drawn together, he remembered how he'd said in the academy, "I don't joke, recruits."

Then he'd looked at the target himself, and seen the holes scattered like a handful of dirt.

"Not what I was expecting, Rowland, even with the finger." Mosley looked at him, beady-eyed. "You can retake it in a week."

"A *week?*"

"You should know by now, Rowland, that I don't make a habit of repeating myself. See you in a week, same day, same place, same time."

He tipped his hat and walked away, shaking his head, leaving Tommy spluttering.

Tommy slammed his fist against the steering wheel before turning out of the shooting range's parking lot. His tires squealed and he grimaced, a bit ashamed of his outward show of emotion. In a move that had recently become as automatic as breathing, he picked up his phone to call Pearl. He cursed again and threw it onto the passenger seat. His relationship with Pearl—a huge distraction—was the primary reason for his failing his shooting test. If he hadn't spent so much time with her and the boys, he would have practiced more.

As Fate would have it, his phone rang at that very minute, and Pearl's name and picture lit up the screen. Even while the sight of her smiling face calmed him, resentment flared up. Not of her, but of himself and his own inability to get done what he needed to. If he'd been more careful of his time, less smitten with Pearl and the boys, he wouldn't have to wait a whole additional week to go back to work.

For the first time since he'd repaired her dishwasher and clothes washer, he let her call go to voicemail. The urge to pick up made his fingers tingle, but he didn't do it. If he was going to get his focus back to where it should be, he was going to have to put some distance between them. In fact, distance was exactly what he needed.

Taking the road that ran north out of town, he turned up his music. Ranch properties, all bare-branched trees and frosty fields dotted with grazing horses, flew by. After several miles and several minutes, his shoulders started to relax and his heartbeat slowed.

After several more miles and several more minutes, he saw his turnoff. The truck trundled down the two-track, and when Tommy looked in the rearview mirror he could see a cloud of dust billowing up behind it.

He wasn't sure he'd be able to find what he was looking for, but then he saw the bales of hay stacked into a tower several yards off the road, sparkling with the carcasses of old aluminum cans. Nostalgia hit him hard as he pulled off the two-track, envisioning all the evenings he'd spent there as a teen, swigging beer and dancing with girls to loud music coming from the speakers on his truck's stereo. Later, he and his friends would go there for target shooting practice, toting gallon-sized milk containers filled with water and all the beer cans they saved up from their parents' (and their own) nights drinking.

"Back to your roots, Tommy boy." He put the truck in park, swung his legs out, and grabbed his gun bag. "You're gonna stay here as long as it takes you to get your mojo back."

Chapter Nineteen

"Good luck today, Abe Lincoln!" Pearl waved goodbye to Wyatt through the open window on the car's passenger side, and he gave her the smallest possible wave before joining a couple of friends who were also dressed up. "Have a good day, Will!" Since he was younger and didn't yet have to impress his friends, Will hollered, "Bye, Mom!" and blew her a kiss.

She sighed, the stress and pressure of the past eighteen hours melting away. "Crisis averted."

As she pulled onto the road, her phone signaled a text message, and her nerve endings prickled at the idea that the message might be from Tommy. She sighed again—this time because she felt so bad that he was experiencing his own crisis.

He'd texted the night before saying he'd failed his shooting test and was going out to practice. The gist of his message: he was too tired and distraught to come over.

Although he didn't say as much, she could read between the lines ... especially because she'd been having similar thoughts. Tommy felt like Pearl (and their time together) had distracted him from practicing like he should. And he'd failed, when passing was as important to him as breathing.

Guilt swamped her when she saw that message, and she hadn't

recovered all night. Sick to her stomach and unable to sleep, she lay in bed with her eyes open and blamed herself for asking too much. He was probably furious at her.

Now, she snatched up her phone to see if he was texting to report he felt better. But no, it was June. Sighing, Pearl rubbed her forehead.

June: *I just heard from Marge at Peaceful Pines. She knows you have a meeting this afternoon,*

Pearl gasped. The meeting! She'd nearly forgotten. She kept reading: *but she wants to make sure you got the photo booth lined up. She heard through the grapevine that Desert Vista also rented a photo booth for their party, which is the same day. She's worried it's the same one.*

The realization dawned on Pearl slowly, like someone poured molasses out of a giant jar and it landed on her head, then slowly, slowly ran down, covering her ears and face and neck.

She'd never reserved the photo booth. And it *was* the only photo booth in town. Which meant that if Desert Vista was using it, Peaceful Pines couldn't.

A sickening *thud* jolted her off that train of thought and her head snapped up. "Oh, shit."

She'd run right into the back of another car. She recognized the maroon hatchback from mornings and afternoons in the drop-off and pick-up line. Her own hood was crumpled, practically folded in half. Smoke or steam (she couldn't quite tell which) flowed upward from her engine.

Frozen in place, she was vaguely aware that the other driver was out of her car and running towards Pearl's door. She knelt down and Pearl whispered, "Emmalita."

Emmalita's motions were fast and jerky as she motioned for Pearl to roll down her window and Pearl complied.

"Are you all right, Pearl?" The woman's forehead was creased in concern. Thank goodness, because if she'd been angry, that would have put Pearl right over the edge.

"I think so." Maybe if she pretended to be faint, she could act like she'd had some kind of medical episode. "Yes, I'm fine."

"What happened?" Emmalita peered into the car, apparently looking for the cause of Pearl's loss of control. Her gaze stopped moving when it landed on Pearl's right hand—and the phone clutched in it. "Were you texting and driving?"

Pearl had known Emmalita for years, since Wyatt and Juan were in kindergarten together, and Emmalita had always been level-headed and funny. But the look that came over her face now was not even close to calm or humorous.

"I forgot to reserve the photo booth."

"What?"

"I forgot to reserve the photo booth. And now the party is going to be a disaster."

"What are you talking about, Pearl? Are you okay? I'm calling an ambulance."

Please do. Please let them take me far away from here, where I don't have to face June or Marge or Rosa or Tommy. I'll live at the hospital if I have to. She closed her eyes and rested her head against the headrest.

"Yes, I need an ambulance at Prescott Gardens Elementary School. There's been a car accident."

"No." Pearl's voice came out in a croaky whisper.

Emmalita covered the mouthpiece with one hand. "What?"

"No, no ambulance. I'm fine. I don't have time for an ambulance. I'm so sorry, Emmalita. I think we need a tow truck, but not an ambulance."

Thank goodness this happened after she dropped the boys off, and not after she picked them up. They weren't here to witness the carnage. Police sirens sounded, and weary, Pearl pushed open her door and hauled herself out of the driver's seat.

Emmalita took her arm, squinting at Pearl because the morning sunlight was shining in her eyes. "Are you okay?"

Quite without warning, Pearl burst into tears. "I'm fine."

They'd never been close—Leslie had discouraged her from having friendships that might distract her from her motherly and wifely duties—but Emmalita wrapped her arms around Pearl, and Pearl cried big, soul-wracking sobs into her shoulder.

The sirens got closer and closer, eventually cutting off when a police cruiser pulled into the parking lot.

"I don't think we need the police, sir," Emmalita said, while Pearl continued to hide her face in the woman's neck. "Just a tow truck, if you don't mind. My friend here is quite distraught and the sooner we can handle this, the better."

A second later, the cop was calling for a tow truck while Emmalita patted Pearl's back and said "shh," and Pearl wondered if she'd worked some kind of witchcraft.

"Can I call someone for you, Pearl?"

Pearl wailed again. She wanted to ask Emmalita to call Tommy, but he was fighting his own demons. "My sister, please. Opal. Actually, I'll call her."

Opal was there within minutes, and the tow truck showed up just after that. Although Pearl's car sustained heavy damage, Emmalita's had barely a scratch on the bumper. Pearl exchanged insurance information with Emmalita and issued several more apologies. As Opal drove her away from the carnage, Pearl's eyes watered anew as she related the story again. "And now I'm going to have to text June back and she's going to be forced to fire me right before Christmas." This exclamation turned into another wail and Opal reached across the cab to put a hand on Pearl's arm.

"I really don't think she's going to fire you, Pearl."

"I forgot to reserve the photo booth! That was my crowning achievement! The feather in my cap! The party is ruined!'

"I don't think the party is ruined. I think you're having a little hiccup, and I'm sure we can find a solution."

"We can't! I have a meeting with the director today! And I'm going to have to tell her. Unless—no, I'm going to have to tell her. There's just not time to find another photo booth."

"Is that the only one in Prescott?"

"The only one I know of. *And*, that Rosa woman is already out to get me if I don't spike the punch! She's looking for a reason to blacklist me."

"Then spike the punch." Opal shrugged and threw a grin her way, but that only made Pearl cry harder.

"I can't! That's got to be illegal, right?"

"Where am I taking you, anyway?"

"I don't even know." The last word came out long and high-pitched, reminding Pearl of one of her boys. "I have so much to do."

"I'm taking you home. Let's talk about what you have to do."

Pearl swiped at the moisture under one eye and started counting on her fingers. "First, I have to respond to June. I still have to finish the snowflakes and centerpieces. I have to pick up the boys and also do Christmas shopping."

"Weren't you and Tommy doing snowflakes and centerpieces the other evening when I called about what size monster slippers to get for Will for Christmas?"

God, Opal was a better aunt than she was a mother. Her Christmas shopping was done. And thinking back on that evening, Pearl cringed. "Yes, but we ... got distracted."

For some inexplicable reason, this put Opal in stitches. She threw her head back and smacked her palm on the steering wheel. "You got distracted! Boy, oh boy, this thing with Tommy is a whole different beast for you, isn't it?" She hooted. "Perfect Pearl would never let a man distract her from an item on her to-do list. I can't tell you how happy this makes me."

Pearl shot her a dark look, which only made her laugh harder.

"So what are we going to do? What's the plan?"

"I *have* no plan! How does a person recover from this?! I still haven't even bought Christmas presents for the boys!"

Much to Pearl's surprise, they'd reached her house, and Opal parked, turned off the car, and turned to face her. "Get it together, Pearl."

Her mouth dropped open. "Did you just tell me to get it together?"

"Yes. Let's go inside. I'll make coffee and you're going to text June and make a plan."

Pearl's body felt like a jointed wooden puppet, stiff and clunky, as she got out of the car and followed Opal inside.

"Sit." Her sister pointed at the dining room table before heading to the coffeemaker. "Text June back now, because I know you're dreading it and you'll feel better once it's done."

Pearl nodded and picked up her phone, but couldn't quite find the words. After letting her thumbs hover over the keyboard for a few long seconds, she typed, *I'm so sorry, June. I forgot to hire the photo booth.* She deleted that. Although she *was* sorry, starting with an apology might sound too whiny. "Better if I present a solution." *Brace yourself. I never reserved the photo booth. I'm such a stupid idiot.* She deleted that, too, and started over: *I hope you're sitting down. I forgot to reserve the photo booth. I am really sorry. It's a rookie mistake, and I'll make it up to you. I'll talk to Marge about it during our meeting and come up with a solution.*

"Have you finished texting her?" The coffeemaker started burbling and Opal came to sit next to Pearl.

She tapped *Send*. "Yes. Just now. I wasn't sure exactly what to say."

"You know what? Stuff goes wrong at June's events all the time. She's said before that putting out fires is one of her biggest responsibilities."

"Yeah, but I *caused* this fire. And I caused it before the event even started."

Opal shrugged. "True. But this is your chance to show her how good you are at firefighting. Don't screw it up."

June's response came through then, short, sweet, and terrifying: *Uh oh.*

"That's it?" Opal said when Pearl reported what June said.

"That's it."

Opal swallowed, the movement audible.

An hour later, caffeinated and focused, Pearl felt somewhat better. Her car was still smashed, but she'd called her insurance company and they were going to provide a rental. First item of business: Opal would take her to pick up the rental car. Next on her list: her meeting with Marge, where she'd have to report that she'd forgotten to reserve the photo booth for the Peaceful Pines holiday party. Then she'd have a couple of hours before picking up the boys, and she could spend that time being crafty.

Chapter Twenty

After failing his shooting test, Tommy ordered himself to take a hiatus from Pearl and the boys. The combination of failing and taking the hiatus made him completely miserable, but after he spent three full hours at the pit—and finally cleared his head enough to get his shooting mojo back—he felt a bit better.

He had only himself to blame for failing the test; he couldn't blame their relationship or his helping Pearl with the boys. If he'd been more serious about practicing, he could have easily taken an hour or two away every day.

But Pearl and the boys were all he was serious about.

Wasn't he the one who always said a guy, especially a cop, needed a family to come home to? A woman and kids or pets, or both, to love? Hadn't he been the one to convince Cash that a guy could have a police career and a good, healthy relationship?

Still, even as he packed up his guns and ammo and cleaned up all this targets, smirking with satisfaction at the neat groupings and obliterated milk containers, he thought that maybe he should slow his roll.

He'd give himself one night away from Pearl and the boys, one night of quiet and solitude to settle back into himself, and then he'd text her in the morning.

His heart still ached at her response to his text about failing his test and needing a little time. She'd simply said, *I understand. Take as much time as you need.*

Really, he should be grateful she hadn't pressed him.

He loaded his gun bag into the backseat and put the targets on the floor. After stopping at the grocery store for supplies, he went home, cooked himself a huge steak and a baked potato, and ate until his stomach ached. Then he drank a single beer, watched the tail end of a football game on TV, and fell into a deep sleep.

He woke up at 5 a.m. in a panic, her text message scrolling through his brain on repeat: *I understand. Take as much time as you need.*

She was feeling the same way he was. Like their relationship was a distraction. She'd forgotten about Wyatt's Abe Lincoln costume (they both had) and she hadn't completed as many of the party-related crafts as she'd wanted to. Not to mention the Christmas-gift situation for the boys. Christmas was still a few days away, but she'd waited too long to order the presents, and barely had time to eat, much less shop.

Why hadn't he seen that he was a distraction for her? He'd ridden in on his high horse, ready to help her, and then fallen in love with her and those boys, believing he was helping them when in fact he was distracting her from her parenting and from a career she was passionate about. "You're a damn fool, Tommy."

Wait. Fallen in love?

He had. He was in love with Pearl Houston.

He was in love with her, and he couldn't let her get away. There was only one way to fix things.

Chapter Twenty-One

Marge Esperanza was a tiny, frail-looking woman with a sharp nose and even sharper eyes. When she offered her hand for a shake and Pearl felt her bony grip tighten, she nearly fell over in fear.

"How are you?" The woman's voice was syrupy sweet and although her eyes crinkled around the corners, her dark irises were cold.

"I'm wonderful." Pearl was certain her voice had never reached that pitch before, and had to stop herself from cringing. "How are you, Marge?"

"Just peachy." She withdrew her hand and straightened up, and despite her short stature, she seemed larger than life. "Now. I'm sure June told you about my concerns about the photo booth. I heard Desert Vista is also getting a photo booth for their holiday party, which is the same day as ours. I just wanted to make sure it's not the same photo booth because, well, you promised us a photo booth and the residents are so looking forward to it. Their spirits would be absolutely broken if you didn't come through. Just crushed."

Pearl's mouth opened. Then it closed. "I—uh—of course it's not the same photo booth. I know how important it is to you guys, and it'll be here for the party."

Oh, my God. What have I just done?

"Oh, wonderful!" Marge's stare finally defrosted and she reached out a bony hand to squeeze Pearl's. "Everyone will be so happy. Rosa has been planning a whole montage of photos with various groups of ladies."

This is like a horror movie. Increasingly zoomed-in images of Rosa's angry face, with a focus on her beady eyes, flashed against Pearl's consciousness while a horror-film slasher sound played.

"Great!"

"Let's go into my office and review everything." Marge motioned for Pearl to follow her, and as they walked through the large social hall, Pearl couldn't help but feel a dozen pairs of eyes watching them.

Sure enough, as soon as they were seated in Marge's office, a cavernous room with generous windows overlooking the facility's park-like grounds, Rosa knocked on the doorframe. "Can I join you ladies?"

Pearl froze.

Marge beamed. "Of course you can, Rosa! Come on in!"

The old woman hobbled into the room and sat down in the chair next to Pearl's. Putting her bony elbows on the arms of the chair, she turned to fix her stare on Pearl, one eyebrow raised. "Got everything ready for the party, Miz Houston?"

Her tone was more threatening than curious, and Pearl's insides constricted. "Of course! It's going to be a wonderful event."

"We're expecting nothing less."

And that wasn't because Rosa had confidence in Pearl; it was, quite obviously, because Rosa and her cronies had a nefarious way of ensuring others met their very high standards. That was the moment Pearl went on autopilot. Her body listened and responded to Marge's comments and questions, and smiled (probably weakly) at Rosa.

But her mind was in deep-thinking mode, racing as fast and hard as possible to come up with a substitute photo booth. If she didn't, Marge and Rosa would know she'd lied. June would find out she'd lied. And she'd actually be blacklisted from ever working in this town again.

Images of her sons scrounging through an empty pantry, their elbows and knees jutting out due to starvation, ran through her mind, obliterating any reasonable thoughts.

Chapter Twenty-Two

"A car accident? Why didn't you tell me?" Tommy nearly sloshed the coffee out of his cup as his heart rate went through the roof.

"I tried! I called you as soon as I heard it on the scanner." Cash was incredulous. "You're the one who didn't pick up, bro. What'd you want me to do, drive over to your house with a memo? Do I need to remind you this is the second time I've called?"

Already in motion, Tommy sped to his bedroom to get dressed. "No, man. Sorry. Thank you for calling. The first and second time." He'd seen Cash's second call only because he was checking his phone to see if Pearl had texted (she hadn't).

"You're welcome. Anyway, sounds like she's having a bit of a rough day."

Opal chimed in from next to Cash. "That's putting it mildly. She also forgot to order the photo booth for the Peaceful Pines Party and had to go admit that to the director over there. Plus, she's still got to get Christmas gifts for the boys. And Baby Isla's party is coming up, too."

Guilt swamping him, he swore. He should never have even considered taking a break from Pearl. She needed him and he hadn't been there for her. "Why didn't she text me?"

"I think she said something about you saying you needed some space and target practice." Opal again, still on speaker. Sometimes this small-town-family thing was great, and sometimes it was a bit too much.

"Right. I did say that. But I didn't mean she couldn't call me in a crisis."

"I'm sure she wanted to."

"Yeah, bro," Cash said. "I'm sure she wanted to. But she was practically having a mental breakdown."

Opal must have elbowed him, or something, because he hissed and said, "What? He deserves to know, doesn't he?"

"She's *fine* now. I made her coffee and she made a list and she went to her meeting with her chin up and a plan to gently let down the Peaceful Pines director and the spiked-punch lady."

"Thanks for the info, you guys. I've got to go." He disconnected, tossed his phone onto his bed, and pulled on his jeans and boots.

On the way out the door, he texted Pearl: *Hey, I know you're still in your meeting, but call me when you're done. We need to talk.*

After sending the message, he realized the last part sounded ominous, and added, *Not talk in a bad way. Talk in a good way.*

Then he headed out, a plan in his mind while his heart waited to hear her voice.

Chapter Twenty-Three

Walking out of her Peaceful Pines meeting, Pearl vowed to herself that she wouldn't look at her phone again for the rest of the day. She turned on her ringer, so she'd know if someone called and she could make sure it wasn't the boys' school. But as a rule, she was keeping it in her purse.

After her disastrous performance, punctuated by a huge lie, she couldn't afford any distractions. She had to figure out a way to get the photo booth to the Peaceful Pines party while also making final preparations for Baby Isla's first birthday party, including the assembly of a giant balloon arch.

Back at June's office, she reviewed the spreadsheet detailing the plans for the birthday party. Fortunately, Callie was a reasonable client who realized the party was more for the adults than it was for the birthday girl, seeing as she was one year old.

"Just make sure there's food, drinks, and music. Oh, and a smash cake."

The spreadsheet showed each vendor—the caterer, the traveling bar, the DJ, and the baker—and listed the communications Pearl received and the day-of party details about arrival, setup, duties, and breakdown.

Reading through it all, Pearl nodded. "At least *this* party's going to go smoothly."

She dashed off quick confirmation emails to all the vendors, and then started an internet search for traveling photo booths. Two were listed in Cottonwood, a small city an hour's drive from Prescott. Maybe, by some miracle, one of them would be available for the Peaceful Pines party.

She dialed the first one. No one picked up, so she left a voicemail and then dialed the second.

"Timeless Memories, this is Jay."

"Hi, Jay, this is Pearl from Sweet Springs Ranch Events over in Prescott. I'm in a bit of a bind and was wondering if you might be able to help me out."

"Hi, Pearl. I'll do my best. Whatcha got?"

"Well, I've got a retirement-home holiday party coming up, and I promised the residents a photo booth. Only, I forgot to reserve it."

"Oh, that sounds like something I can help with. When is this party?"

Pearl closed her eyes. "Day after tomorrow."

A beat of silence passed while Jay digested the information. "Yeah, so, Pearl. I'm so sorry to say I'm not going to be able to help you out with that. It's a weekend in December, which means I'm booked solid for holiday parties."

"I was afraid of that."

"You tried Picture Perfect?"

She swallowed. "I called, but no answer. Left a message."

"Okay. I mean, you could try calling some places in Phoenix? Some of those bigger outfits have more than one booth."

"Good idea. Thanks for your help."

Nausea roiling in her stomach, she took Jay's advice and expanded her search to the Phoenix area. As he'd said, there were lots of photo booth companies there. She checked her watch. Because she'd have to get the boys soon, she didn't have time to call every single company. Working quickly, she whipped up an email she could copy and paste—going for urgent but not desperate—and sent it out to as many as she could in the ten minutes she had left.

Then she sent up a prayer, packed up her things, and left to get the boys.

When she arrived at the school, she had to roll down her window and wave so they'd recognize her in the rental car. When she explained why she was driving it, Wyatt threw his entire body back against the seat and closed his eyes in a dramatic display of embarrassment.

"That was *you?* We heard about the crash during recess. Jada Montgomery was late to school and saw the whole thing." He threw his hands over his eyes. "Oh, my God. Now that I know it was you, this is even worse. You were the hysterical one, right? The one who crashed into the back of Juan's mom's car? The one who cried as Juan's mom comforted you? Oh, my gawwwwd."

At any other time, Pearl would have found this conversation comical, but it was just proof she was failing on all fronts. Something snapped inside her, and she saw red. She gave him her best fraction-of-a-second glare in the rearview mirror, then focused on the road again, that morning's accident still fresh in her mind. "You know what, Wyatt? You kids aren't the only ones allowed a bad day, okay? Moms have bad days, too, but we're not allowed to talk about it. We're supposed to put on a happy face All. The. Time. Well, you know what, you guys?" Another glance in the rearview mirror revealed both her boys' wide-eyed expressions. She plowed on. "I'm having a bad week. I had to panic and rush to get your Abe Lincoln costume. I haven't finished the snowflakes or the centerpieces for the Peaceful Pines party, or the balloon arch for Isla's party. I forgot to order the photo booth, for God's sake. And you know why? Because for the first time in ages, I was smitten with a *man!* I was smitten with a man who was so good to me, so good to you, that I let all my responsibilities take the backseat." Her chest heaved and her arms shook with emotion. "I forgot to order your Christmas presents! And even though Christmas isn't here yet, nothing will arrive in time and I don't know when I'm going to go shopping and Christmas is ruined! *Ruined!*"

If Wyatt and Will's eyes were round before her tirade, they were saucers as she clapped a hand over her mouth. She hadn't meant to tell them that part.

"Mom?" Will leaned forward, his hand on the back of her seat. For the second time that day, she was wishing with all her might that she could take back something she'd said.

"Yeah?" She licked her lips, wishing with all her might that Will wasn't going to say anything that would make her feel even guiltier than she already did.

"Christmas isn't ruined. It's okay. I'm not going to say we don't care about presents, because we do." Pearl heard the swoosh of skin on seat fabric, and the *thump* of an elbow connecting with an upper arm. Then Will said, "Ow, Wyatt. Don't act all *perfect*. We care about presents. But let me finish."

"Fine. Geez."

"But we know you've been working so hard on these parties so you can get an even better job and take even better care of us. And we *love* having Mr. Tommy around. He got us a tree, which is also part of Christmas. He helped us decorate. We've all been watching Christmas movies." Pearl's eyes started to prickle with tears. "You know how you always say you love the holiday season because it's all warm and fuzzy?"

Unable to speak, she nodded.

"Well, that's why we love it, too. And we still have that."

She reached back to squeeze his hand. "Thank you, buddy. That means a lot."

"You're still gonna get us presents, though, right? They just might be late?"

A sobbing laugh escaped. "Right."

"We understand, Mom," Wyatt said. "But maybe you can ask Santa to bring us a little something extra for making us wait." He winked at her in the rearview mirror, an action so adult, she wanted to cry.

They'd nearly reached home and Pearl sat up straighter when she saw Tommy's truck parked along the curb.

"Mr. Tommy's here!" Wyatt was unbuckling and throwing open his door, and Pearl hadn't even parked her car yet.

Will hollered and followed along, and Pearl rushed to stop so she didn't run them over. By the time she got her wits about her and got out of the car, Tommy had wrapped her two boys in a giant bear hug and they were laughing with glee.

As she walked up the sidewalk, her eyes met his and she actually felt the gratitude and love—yes, love—rush through her body, and ethereal tingling.

"Boys! Empty the backseat, please. Bring everything inside. And, hurry. Be quick about it. There's an alien invasion underway and we've got to saddle our dragons."

Still giggling and rolling their eyes with amusement, they fell away from him and rushed to open the truck's back doors. Tommy strode toward Pearl slowly, but with purpose burning in his eyes— the kind of purpose that at once turned her on and melted her heart.

He was here because he cared about her. Yes, he'd failed his shooting test. Yes, he'd taken a little time away. But he'd come back.

"Hi." He wrapped his arms around her waist.

"Hi." She wrapped hers around his shoulders.

Their lips met and that ethereal tingling feeling spread from her torso to her fingers and toes, warming her from within.

"How are you?" he wanted to know, his mouth just a breath from hers.

"Better now that you're here."

"Will you be even better when you find out I brought dinner?"

"I think I'm in love." She blurted it out, and although she didn't wish she could take back these words, she hoped she hadn't said too much.

But all he did was groan, pull her waist tight against his so she could feel his arousal, and kiss her again. "I also brought scissors and my own hot glue gun so I could help you with the snowflakes and centerpieces. And whatever else you need."

"You're amazing."

"I know."

Inside, he put the giant lasagna in the oven and then told the boys, "No running off to your rooms when you're done putting away those groceries. We're going to help your mom with these snowflakes." Just as Will inhaled to argue, Tommy held up a finger. "No complaining. This is family business."

"Pearl."

"Yes, Tommy." Her lips twitched.

His eyes twinkled. "Let's make us a good, old-fashioned assembly line for these snowflakes."

She nodded, brushed her hands together, and then got to work, setting the blank paper at one end of the table, the glue and glitter in the middle, and the yarn at the end.

With Pearl cutting, Tommy gluing, Wyatt glittering, and Will tying (much to his dismay), they had plowed through dozens of the snowflakes when Tommy said, "So, are you all ready for the Peaceful Pines party?"

Pearl had almost let herself forget about the whole photo booth debacle by the time the lasagna finished cooking.

"Welllll, she forgot to order the photo booth." Will was bent over his snowflake, tying on a piece of string to hang it up. "So there's that."

For the first time when it came to that situation, Pearl laughed. "I forgot to order the photo booth. Which reminds me. I've stopped obsessing over my email, but I do need to check and see if any of the Phoenix-based ones have emailed me back."

Only then did she look at Tommy, who was obviously doing his best not to look alarmed. "I mean, I'm sure it's fine if you don't have the photo booth, right? It's just one thing. You've got the snowflakes." He held one up. "You're going to have the centerpieces. And by golly, I can run to the store and make sure you have enough rum to at least spike that one lady's punch, keep her happy."

The anxiety rolling back in, Pearl sighed. "There's one more problem, though."

"What's that?"

Everyone froze, looking at her.

"I told Marge, today, that I'd reserved it. I told her it was no problem, that of course we'd have a photo booth." All the words she'd been thinking but not saying came tumbling out of her mouth. "It was so stupid. I don't know why I did it. Well, I mean, I do know why. I did it because I was desperate. Because I want this party to turn out great. Because if it does, I'll get more work with June, and I'll be able to do so much for the boys. But I was an idiot. There's almost no way I can snag a photo booth at this late hour, especially on a weekend during December."

Without waiting for anyone to respond, she got up and went to the kitchen to retrieve her phone. Her heart leapt when she saw a few replies to her spate of emails earlier, but it quickly settled back down when she realized they all said pretty much the same thing Jay from Timeless Memories said: it was a no go.

Head hanging, she returned to the dining room table, where the boys did their best to console her with funny stories and silly antics until they ate lasagna and moved on to centerpieces. Maybe she'd messed this up enough that she wouldn't get the bigger job with June, but at least she'd always have her little family.

Chapter Twenty-Four

Tommy knew as soon as he saw Pearl and the boys returning home that evening: he was right where he was supposed to be.

The boys ran right up to him like they hadn't seen him in months, even though it had been a couple of days. And Pearl's smile when she spotted him was pure magic. Although their routine, their dynamic, had seemed so natural before that he almost hadn't noticed it, that evening he realized how special it was.

He hugged the boys and then asked them to pitch in with grocery transport, and they'd done it as if following his instructions was second nature. And when they'd all sat down to work on the snowflakes and talk about the day, he'd loved every minute of hearing about Wyatt's Abe Lincoln presentation and Will's new trick on the monkey bars and the pig that showed up at the school assembly.

Seeing Pearl relaxed and at ease (at least until they'd mentioned the photo booth) in the glowing lights from the Christmas tree made him feel so content, he was overcome with a desire to ensure she felt relaxed and at ease all the time.

The longer they sat there, the more he realized that evenings like that were exactly what he wanted—every evening, week after week, month after month, year after year. Forever.

He was dying to tell her. But he couldn't—not just yet. He had to wait until after her two big parties, after his second shooting test, after they'd both put their stressors behind them. Instead, after they took turns reading pages of the boys' favorite Christmas story, put the boys to bed, brought them each another glass of water, and hollered, "Go to sleep," several more times, he pulled her onto the couch, gathered her into his arms, kissed the top of her head, and held her.

"Thank you for all your help. I would have been up all night tomorrow night trying to finish everything."

"You're welcome."

"Now I just have to deal with the balloon arch and the Christmas present situation. I can't believe I can't get stuff shipped in time. I'm never waiting until the last minute again."

"We could go shopping right now, finish the balloons when we get home."

"And leave the boys?"

Tommy shrugged. "Yeah. I used to stay home alone all the time at Wyatt's age. We could just tell him he's the man of the house for a couple of hours, and I'll bet he'd love it. Oh, and we could leave my phone here so he can call us if there's an emergency."

"You've thought of everything. Except, what if he ends up playing games on your phone the whole time we're gone?"

"Then he'll be real tired tomorrow—but at least you'll have presents for them. I don't have any good games on my phone, anyway. Just a vintage Pac-Man game."

"*That's* the game you have on your phone?"

He shrugged again. "Yeah. I'm very busy and important. I don't have time for games."

Without warning, she got to her feet. "This is a great idea. Let's go. I'll go talk to Wyatt."

"Should I come with you, so I can show him how to open my phone?"

"You're full of good ideas." She offered both hands and pulled him to his feet, then wrapped her arms around his waist and brought him in for a kiss, which made him wish he wasn't such a good guy—he'd happily stay home and take the kissing to the next level if he didn't care so much about getting gifts for Wyatt and Will.

"If that's how you're going to thank me, I'll keep having good ideas."

"Please do."

They kissed again, and Tommy felt himself going hard against her body. "We'd better stop, or we're not going to make it to the store."

"Fair enough."

He was glad to see the disappointment on her expression mirrored his. They tiptoed down the hall and into Wyatt's room.

"What are you guys doing?"

"We have a favor to ask," Tommy said. "We're going to go run an errand." He winked at Wyatt, and understanding dawned on the kid's face right away.

"And you want me to hold down the fort."

"Exactly."

"No problem."

Tommy could literally feel the electric jolt of surprise surge through Pearl's body. Although he wanted to ruffle Wyatt's hair, he thought the moment called for a slightly more grown-up gesture, and he squeezed his upper arm. "Thank you, man. We're going to leave my phone so you call if there's an emergency. We'll be ten minutes away, max."

"And if you need to, you can use your police driving skills and be here in five."

"Ha." He glanced at Pearl. "I could. Not sure if we should tell your mom that, though."

Wyatt grinned, and Tommy knew in that instant, he'd do anything for him.

"Let me show you the code to open my phone, and where the phone app is. I'll call your mom's phone now so she's first on the list, and all you have to do is tap her name."

He nodded. "Okay."

Tommy showed him the code and the phone app. His face heated just a bit. "Actually, your mom is already first on the list."

"Aw, how cute." Sarcasm coated the words, and Tommy felt another rush of affection.

"Watch it, man. Are you all right for a couple of hours? Think you can just go to sleep?"

"I'm fine, man." He swiped a dismissive hand at them. "Go on, get outta here."

In the car, a shivering Pearl said, "Wow, I can't believe how nonchalant he was about staying home. I've never seen him so brave."

"It's all the time he's been spending around me." Tommy winked at her as he turned on the engine, and although he was joking, she nodded.

"I think you're right. The only message my ex gave the boys was that they weren't good enough at anything or for anything. You interact with them so differently, you've given them confidence."

Tommy felt like he could float. He grinned at Pearl as he backed out of the driveway.

With Christmas just days away, the big box store bustled, even at this late hour.

"Wow. I can't believe how many people are here." Pearl sat up straighter and looked around as Tommy found a parking spot at the far end of the lot.

"Me, neither. But I guess everybody has the same idea—get their shopping in while the kids sleep."

Inside, the energy was frenetic as people filled their carts and vied for those remaining in-demand items.

Tommy cracked his knuckles and stretched his neck, making Pearl laugh. "Where should we start, Milady?"

"Toys. I know I want to get them both LEGO sets. And then books. I like to get each of them a book." As soon as they rounded the corner, Pearl gasped. "That's the dragon set I've been wanting to get Will. C'mon. There's only one left."

Her enthusiasm was adorable and contagious and they reached the shelf just as another young guy did. He and Pearl reached for the box at the same time. Tommy expected the guy to be polite and let Pearl have it, but he didn't loosen his grip—and neither did Pearl. Tommy had never seen that competitive edge in her eyes before, and he liked it.

"Look," Pearl said to the guy, who sported a thick blond mustache. "I'm having a really bad week. It would mean a lot to me if I could check this Christmas gift off my list."

The guy shrugged, his upper lip (and mustache) bending into a sneer. "Not my problem you're having a bad week, lady. I've been looking for this set for weeks. Been to five different stores."

"You want it for *yourself?*" Pearl's eyebrows shot up and she pulled the box toward her chest.

"So what if I do?" He pulled the box toward his chest.

"This is going to be for a six-year-old *kid!*"

Tommy stepped forward. "May I interject?"

Both Pearl and the other guy looked at him, their heads snapping in his direction. "No."

At that, he laughed out loud and held up his hands in surrender. "Okay." While they continued to argue over the LEGO set, Pearl reasoning that the guy could buy it for himself after Christmas, since he was an adult, and the guy arguing that he was buying it for himself for Christmas, Tommy pulled out his phone. Within a few minutes, he'd found another dragon LEGO set at a store two hours away. He ordered it, had it shipped to their local store with delivery by December 23, and placed a hand on Pearl's arm just as she was saying, "I'll fight you for it!"

This had all three of them laughing, and when Tommy could finally catch a breath, he said, "Let him have it."

Her eyebrows drew downward and her chest heaved as she inhaled, preparing to argue, but he gave her arm a little squeeze and said, "I found another one. It'll be at this store for pickup two days before Christmas."

"Oh." Her entire being deflated and she released the box.

Her adversary hugged it like it was a long lost friend, and then threw his arms around Tommy. "Thank you, man. I've wanted this set since I was fifteen, but could never afford it for myself until now."

Tommy patted his back. "You're welcome. Merry Christmas."

"Merry Christmas, bro."

As if he was worried Pearl might snatch it back, he tucked the box under his arm and hoofed it toward the front of the store. Once again, Pearl dissolved into laughter.

"Were you really planning to fight him for it?" Tommy looked at her sideways, which only made her laugh harder.

"No. I was half-joking, but I wanted him to know how serious I was about Will opening that dragon set on Christmas morning."

Tommy shook his head, half amused with Pearl and half amused with himself for letting that whole interaction make him fall even more in love with her.

Chapter Twenty-Five

On the morning of Baby Isla's first birthday party, Pearl woke with flutters of anticipation in her stomach. The party wasn't as big or as important as the Peaceful Pines shindig, but if it turned out well, she'd gain some emotional momentum, which was just what she needed.

And, if the Wilder family was impressed enough, she'd gain some practical momentum: they were big in town, and their referrals and recommendations certainly wouldn't hurt her fledgling career.

The coffeemaker finished its brew just as she padded into the kitchen, shivering at the chill in the air. After pouring herself a cup of coffee, which she'd made especially strong the night before, she turned on the Christmas tree lights and the fireplace, and sat down to check her email one more time. Her hopes weren't too high. Every single photo booth owner who had responded to Pearl's queries was booked on the date of the Peaceful Pines holiday party. Those who hadn't responded likely figured she didn't warrant an answer, since she was so idiotic as to forget to book such a significant service during the busiest-of-busy holiday season.

But she couldn't focus on that today. She closed her laptop, closed her eyes, and took a deep breath. Today, she had to shift her attention to Baby Isla's birthday party.

Two hours later, she arrived at Callie and Hayes's house, her backseat and trunk loaded to the gills with supplies and decorations. A moment after she pulled in, another car did, too. She waved when she recognized Callie's sister-in-law, Lila, and Lila came over to give her a hug.

"I told Callie I'd help out this morning, since June's out of commission and Opal's watching your boys until Tommy relieves her."

"Then I guess I'd better put you to work."

When Pearl popped her trunk, Lila staggered backwards, her hand over her heart in faux shock. "Callie said this was a low-key, small function."

Pearl laughed. "It is. But June said that when clients say that, the details are even more important." She gestured at the bins and totes and bags. "Hence, details."

Callie came out just as Pearl and Lila had each gathered a load, and she whistled long and low. "Wow. I thought this was going to be a low-key, small function."

"It is," Pearl said, even though her confidence was quickly waning. "Just wait and see."

A while later, after the three of them had carried everything into the house, Pearl told them she'd handle the decorating if they wanted to relax.

"Oh, no," Callie said. "I've got to put in some of the work. If you do everything, what will I tell Isla when she's grown and has a child of her own? 'Honey, I didn't put any effort at all into your first birthday party.' No, I've got to slave away, at least a little. Tell me what to do, Pearl. This is your show."

And just like that, Pearl was thrust into the driver's seat for her very first event. She assigned jobs to both Callie and Lila, and acted like she knew what she was doing when the caterer and the baker showed up. Every time her confidence faltered, she threw her shoulders back, lifted her chin, and made a decision.

Thirty minutes before the party was set to begin, all the vendors had left and she, Callie, and Lila stood in the pristine kitchen, where the food was laid out alongside pitchers of lemonade and iced tea.

"Wow, Pearl. You've really worked some magic, here." Callie slipped an arm around Pearl's waist and squeezed. "This will be a party Isla will never remember." They all cackled at that. "But seriously, Hayes and I will remember it, which is what matters. It'll be a lovely day when everyone in our lives comes together to celebrate our baby girl. And I didn't have to stress over it, not even a little, because I knew you had things under control."

Pearl beamed, and that glow stayed with her as guests arrived. She circulated throughout the party, refilling food platters, cleaning up little spills, throwing away tiny disposable plates and cups, and making sure everyone signed the guest book. When Isla opened her gifts (with the help of her parents), Pearl wrote down who'd given what, so Callie could write thank-you notes on the cards Pearl had already purchased. When it was time for Isla to smash her cake, Pearl laid a disposable tablecloth on her high chair tray for easy cleanup. When the party dwindled, Pearl thanked each guest for coming.

She couldn't help but overhear little comments—compliments that made her heart sing.

"Pearl thought of everything."

"This is the best party I've been to in a long time."

"I love the decorations. They're the cutest and so unique."

"The food is so good, and it hasn't run out all afternoon."

At one point, Opal came up to her as she added ice to the iced tea dispenser and whispered, "You're amazing at this, Pearl, and I'm not just saying so because I'm your sister."

And June, Remington in one arm, pulled her aside and was nearly jumping with excitement. "This is perfect, Pearl. I couldn't have done it better, myself. You've pulled it off, and I'm so proud of you."

I'm doing it. I'm running an event I organized, and I'm pulling it off. By the time the last guest left and she stood in the empty living room with Callie, Hayes, and a tired and cranky Isla, Pearl was completely knackered—and also completely relieved.

"Happy birthday, Isla," she said to the baby, who babbled at her for approximately a half-second before twisting in her father's arms.

"She says thank you, Auntie Pearl," Callie said, and Hayes said, "I'm going to put her down for a nap. Be right back."

Once they were gone, Callie turned to Pearl and grabbed her hands. "Thank you. So much. That was absolutely wonderful. I definitely couldn't have pulled it off without you, and also, even if I did manage to pull off a party, it wouldn't have been nearly as amazing. I'm pretty sure you just launched your career as an event planner, Pearl Houston."

She floated out of the house, down the driveway, and into her car, only to remember that she still had to show up at the Peaceful Pines party the next day—with some kind of explanation about why there wouldn't be a photo booth.

If only she could stop the slow deflating of her spirits, but she couldn't. As she drove home, she could feel herself getting smaller in the driver's seat, all the confidence from the past several hours dissolving into the air around her.

Then she saw Tommy standing outside of her house with the boys, who waved wildly at her, as if she'd been gone for months rather than hours.

Everything will be okay. If all else fails, I've got two wonderful sons and an amazing ... boyfriend?

Giving Tommy a title tripped her up momentarily, but she recovered quickly as she realized the title didn't matter. She parked and jumped out of the car, then ran over to hug them.

"How'd it go?"

"Mr. Tommy! Tell her!" Will pulled on Tommy's hand.

"Tell me what?" She grimaced. "Did you guys break something? I've been telling you not to roughhouse inside."

Wyatt cackled. "Mo-om. We didn't break anything."

Pearl's attention returned to Tommy, who looked fidgety. "We have something to show you."

Wyatt and Will each grabbed one of her hands to lead her down the sidewalk. "Where are we going?"

"You'll see," Wyatt said, bordering on hysteria.

They stopped next to a little camping trailer Pearl hadn't even noticed. It was parked along the street and even if she had noticed it, she'd have assumed one of her neighbors was packing it for a trip. Awareness started to dawn, prickling at the edge of her consciousness.

With a flourish, Tommy said, "We present to you the Sweet Springs Events traveling photo booth."

Her mouth dropped open and she whirled to look at him. The boys clung to her hands, awaiting her reaction.

"What—how—when—"

"Are you excited, Mommy?" Will tugged on her.

"I'm completely flabbergasted," she admitted. "And yes, I'm excited. Very excited. And I have so many questions."

"Mr. Tommy did most of the work," Wyatt said, matter-of-fact. "He brought it over this morning, since you were already gone."

"And we helped him with the finishing touches," Will said.

She looked at Tommy, whose shoulders were tense as he waited for her reaction to come around. He shrugged, cleared his throat. "When you told me about the photo booth conundrum, I remembered that my parents had this old trailer sitting on their property. I was still off work—maybe it was a blessing in disguise—and I thought, hey, I could fix that up." A beat of silence passed and then he said, "Well, do you want to see it?"

Of course she wanted to see it, but first she had to give him a proper thank you. She squeezed the boys' hands before letting them go, then launched herself at Tommy, who caught her with a surprised bark of laughter.

"Thank you so much," she said, her mouth close to his ear. "This is seriously the nicest thing anybody has ever done for me." He set her down and she straightened her sweater. "I mean, you already did the other nicest thing anybody has ever done for me, by fixing my stuff and helping with the boys. But you've outdone yourself, Tommy Rowland."

Smiling, he said, "*Now* do you want to see it?"

"Yes!"

"Boys! Give her the tour!"

Tears sprang to her eyes at that—not only had he made the most wonderful grand gesture to help her in her time of need, but he'd involved the boys and now he was stepping aside at the climax to let them share in the glory.

The boys took the lead and Pearl wrapped an arm around Tommy's waist as they followed. "You're a wonderful man, you know that?"

His eyes shone as he looked down at her. "I mean, yeah. But I don't mind hearing it from you."

Delighted, she laughed. The boys clambered up the trailer steps and Tommy gestured for Pearl to go in ahead of him. She loved what she saw: at one end, he'd put in a bench seat where people would pose for their photos, and on the other side, he'd set up a tripod. There were cute pillows on the bench and little signs on the walls: *Smile! You look great! Say cheese!*

"This is perfect. I would say I can't believe you pulled this off, but if anyone could do it, it's you."

"I *am* pretty amazing. And I had help."

"I hung up the signs," Wyatt said, chest out with pride.

"And I cleaned all the windows and the floor," Will said.

"Oh, so you know how to clean stuff now? I'll keep that in mind."

"Mo-om."

"Thank you, all, so much." She gathered the boys in her arms, hugging them until they squealed to be let go, and then they dashed out of the trailer, across the lawn, and into the house, leaving Pearl and Tommy alone.

"I don't know if I can ever adequately thank you for this." She took his hands in hers. "You singlehandedly saved my career."

He looked at her sternly. "I doubt that. I came through in an emergency, but I'm confident you would have saved your career on your own."

"But I didn't have to. And that's worth a million thanks."

"You can start paying me back tonight after the boys go to bed."

"Oh, trust me. I plan on it."

Chapter Twenty-Six

It was the best Christmas Eve Tommy could remember in a long time. He and Pearl had taken the boys over to the Sweet Springs Ranch for a giant Christmas feast with the Wilders, and they'd all basked in the warm glow of family—the joking and laughing and teasing and eating. Even cleaning up had somehow been warm and cozy, and then they all sat around the tree and opened gifts.

By 9 p.m., the living room of the big house was the definition of chaos, with wrapping paper and gift bags and ribbon strewn all over the place and Pearl's kids sprawled on the rug, chattering away about their presents.

The adults sat at the dining table sipping hot cocoa, watching the kids. Tommy sat next to Pearl, his hand on her thigh, her shoulder against his. He could stand a million more evenings exactly like this one.

June, Remington sleeping on her chest, wiped a tear off her cheek. "You know, I can't help but think this evening is bringing this old house back to life. I can feel it. This is what it was built for, isn't it? It was built as a gathering place for family, for brothers and sisters and friends and children."

One of the kids shrieked, and everyone laughed.

Pearl, too, wiped a tear from her cheek. "You can feel the house coming alive. I feel myself coming alive, too, thanks to you guys including the boys and me in this family."

"This big, wild, crazy family," Sterling said.

"It's a wonderful family," Pearl said.

Hearing her contentment, see how relaxed she was—and knowing her contentment matched his—cemented a decision he'd made earlier that week. He'd decided he wanted to be with Pearl, and with the boys, for the rest of his life.

Pearl rested her head on his shoulder, almost as if she could hear his thoughts.

Suddenly, he couldn't wait to get home with her, so they could get to bed and wake up together on Christmas morning.

"I suppose we should call it a night," he said to her, and she sat up, nodding.

"Those boys are going to be up before dawn tomorrow."

With minimal protests, Wyatt and Will helped clean up the gift wrap, said good-bye to the Wilder family, and carried their gifts to the truck.

Because they believed they weren't getting any gifts the next day, they went to bed easily and without fuss, and after they fell asleep, Tommy and Pearl snuck into her bedroom to do the last-minute gift wrapping and stocking stuffing. Then, working together, they brought all the gifts out to the living room and placed them under the tree. They stood back to admire their work.

"Looks pretty awesome to me," Tommy said.

Pearl nodded. "They're going to be so surprised. And even though it's late, I feel like we should sit out here for a while with the Christmas tree lights on."

"I agree. Want a night cap?"

"Sure. But I don't know if we have anything to make cocktails with."

"I have just the thing. When the boys and I went to the store yesterday, I bought the supplies for a Naughty but Nice cocktail."

He'd never tire of seeing the surprise and delight in her eyes when he did something nice for her.

"Is that a prelude to my thanking you for the photo booth?"

He laughed. "I hadn't thought of that, but yes, it could be. Definitely."

A few minutes later they settled on the couch, cocktails in hand, the sparkling tree lights reflecting off the gifts, the fireplace roaring.

"I think this is my favorite Christmas ever," Tommy said, and Pearl laughed. "It's not even Christmas yet."

"Christmas is a season, Pearl."

She laughed, and the sound felt like medicine to his soul. "You're right. And you know what? It's my favorite Christmas ever, too. I still can't believe you pulled off that photo booth. And I still can't believe I pulled off the Peaceful Pines party without a hitch. Did I tell you Marge and Rosa both told me they're going to tell everyone they know they should hire me for event planning?"

"That's awesome. You didn't tell me that—I think you were more interested in telling me how you brought Rosa her own flask of spiked punch. A sparkly flask, no less."

"Ha. I also can't believe I did that."

"You know what? I can believe all of it. You're a special woman, Pearl. You'll do what it takes to make things work, to take care of the boys. I'm confident you can do anything you set your mind to. And that's why I love you."

She stilled. "You love me?"

"I do. I've been afraid to say it. But now I've had a drink and I pulled off the photo booth, and, to be honest, I'm pretty sure you love me, too."

Another laugh. "You're right. I love you, too, Tommy Rowland."

They kissed then, a long, slow, lingering kiss that warmed Tommy more than the cocktail possibly could.

"I'm glad."

They sat in silence for a little while, sipping their cocktails while also letting their hands roam over each other's bodies. He ran a palm up and down her thigh, and she stroked the length of him through his pajama pants.

By the time he drained his glass, he was incredibly turned on. "You almost done with your Naughty but Nice?"

"Why, you want to go be naughty but nice?"

"Um, yeah. And I believe you have some thanking me to do."

"You know what?" She drained her glass. "You're right. Let's go."

She got up and headed for the bedroom, dropping her pants and throwing off her shirt as he followed her.

Chapter Twenty-Seven

Pearl woke before the kids on Christmas morning—a first since they were both old enough for the anticipation to wake them well before dawn. Trying not to wake Tommy, she slipped out of bed and went into the kitchen to get coffee. She put cinnamon rolls in the oven, turned on the Christmas tree lights, and sat down in the otherwise dark living room.

Just as she had the night before, she admired hers and Tommy's handiwork. The gifts they'd bought and wrapped for the boys sat neatly under and around the tree, almost magical in the glow.

She turned at the sound of approaching footsteps, and smiled when Tommy grinned at her.

"Merry Christmas."

"Merry Christmas to you." He bent down to kiss her. "Coffee. Be right back."

A moment later, he sat down next to her, their bodies touching from shoulder to ankle. "This is my first Christmas with kids—well, since I was a kid—and it's way more fun than Christmas with adults."

"I know. There's something magical about Christmas with kids. Although, if you're Rosa from Peaceful Pines, and you've got a flask full of spiked punch, Christmas with adults is a pretty darn good time."

Tommy chuckled. "I can't believe you brought her the spiked punch."

"I'll tell you what. I can't, either. But I think, along with your photo booth, which was a huge hit, that spiked punch made the party. Rosa in her knackered state definitely leveled things up."

"That's hilarious. I wish I'd been there to see it, but I definitely got a kick out of the pictures."

From the hallway came the sounds of Wyatt getting out of bed. His footsteps moved through his bedroom and across the hall. He knocked on Will's door. "It's Christmas!"

A flurry of activity followed, Will pushing back his covers, jumping out of bed, and running to his door, and then both boys scurrying down the hall to the living room, where they skidded to a halt when they saw the presents.

"Presents!" They threw their arms around each other and jumped around in a circle. Pearl's throat tightened. They'd been so mature about the potential lack of gifts, and their reaction now only proved how much they'd cared about her feelings.

Only after a few gleeful seconds did they realize Pearl and Tommy were in the room. Their dance continued, right over to the couch. They clambered on, wrapping their arms around both adults, shouting, "Merry Christmas" on repeat.

"I think we should have some breakfast before we open gifts, though," Pearl said as the hugs subsided.

"Aw, Mom, do we have to?" Will's lower lip jutted out.

Wyatt elbowed him. "'Course we do. Mom makes us wait every year because she likes the morning to last a little longer."

"All right, all right."

"Why don't you boys serve the breakfast?" Tommy said, and Pearl fell a little more in love with him in that moment.

In the smallest ways, he was showing them what it meant to be part of a family, to contribute, to grow into wonderful men. Of course, partly because he'd suggested it and partly because they were anxious to get to the present-opening, they hopped to it and brought out the cinnamon rolls for everyone to enjoy. Without being asked, they also took the empty plates back to the kitchen.

Pearl raised an eyebrow at Tommy, who simply smiled. God, how she loved this thing between them, how they shared these tiny moments in the midst of all the chaos. Wasn't that what real, deep, everlasting love was all about?

The boys thundered back in, ready to tear into their bounty. When they were done a mere thirty minutes later (five solid minutes of which were spent with Will hollering in excitement over the dragon LEGO set), Tommy sat back on the couch and sighed. "Wow. That happened way faster than I expected. You put all this time into buying presents and wrapping them, and it's all over in minutes!"

"I know. It's crazy, isn't it?"

"So crazy. But so fun."

"Will you guys help us set up this airplane?" Wyatt held up the giant model airplane Tommy had bought them.

"We will," Tommy said, "but first your mom has to open her present."

Pearl sat up straight, indignant. "I thought we agreed we weren't going to buy each other Christmas gifts."

Tommy flashed her a cunning smile. "It's not a Christmas gift. It's just a gift, and it just happens I bought it around Christmas time."

"What is it?" The boys started again with their jumping, and Pearl laughed.

"Settle down, you two."

"I'll be right back." Tommy went into the bedroom and returned with a small gift bag, which he handed to Pearl before sitting next to her again.

She removed the tissue paper and peered inside, where a black velvet jewelry box sat snugly in another sheet of tissue. Her heartbeat picked up. She glanced at Tommy, and his Adam's apple bobbed. The box felt soft and high quality against her fingers as she removed it.

"Open it, Mom!" Will bounded over and hopped up next to her on the couch.

"I am!" And when she did, her heart danced. From inside the box, a diamond ring sparkled up at her. She looked at Tommy again, an eyebrow raised.

He cleared his throat. "Since I first laid eyes on you last year, I thought you were special. And really good-looking." The boys laughed at that. "And since we started spending more time together, I've realized you *are* special. Beyond special. And not just because you're good-looking." Another snicker from the boys. "You're so strong, Pearl, and so determined. You're fun and funny and a wonderful mom. And you're great in the ..." he raised an eyebrow at her and she smiled back. "Kitchen. Anyway. I realized recently that I want to spend every single day with you, for the rest of our lives. I want to wake up next to you, go to bed next to you, eat dinner around the table with you and the boys. I want the soccer games and sword fights and even the late-night shopping. I want all of it. I want all of you."

She felt her eyes filling with tears.

"Will you marry me, Pearl?"

She glanced at Wyatt and Will, and they both nodded, eyebrows raised in encouragement.

"He already asked us, Mama," Wyatt said.

Her entire body flooded with gratitude and love, and she leaned in to kiss Tommy, who took the box out of her hands.

"So, will you?"

She laughed and cried, nodding, and he took the ring out of the box and slipped it onto her finger. And she thought, *This is how happily ever after begins.*

The End

About the Author

Hilary Dartt loves great adventures, whether she's writing, reading, or living them. The author of twelve novels, Hilary lives in Arizona's high desert with her husband, their three children, and her Weimaraner, Leia. She loves camping, exploring in the Jeep, and dance parties with her kids. Learn more and sign up for her newsletter at www.hilarydartt.com.

www.ingramcontent.com/pod-product-compliance
Lightning Source LLC
Chambersburg PA
CBHW021713190726
48289CB00008B/2504